SINS OF THE DAMNED

Elisium: Book 2

ELENA LAWSON

I

"What happened to your mercy?" I mouth the words along with Fernand, tracing the line of the Count's face on the beveled screen of the ancient television in Kincaid's basement.

"I'm a count," I say with Edmond Dantes. "Not a saint."

I grin as a weight comes off my chest but buckle a moment later as another heavier one settles in its place. There's not very much resemblance between them, so then why does this movie remind me so much of him?

It could be the resemblance between him and the character of Albert Modego, played by a young Henry Cavil perhaps? Or it could be the blind fury and singular focus on retribution—the same as the fire that burns at a constant behind the eyes of my Lord of the Underworld.

"Not this again," Artemis whines, stepping heavily on the last two stairs leading down to the old cellar-like basement. "If you don't turn that thing off soon and stop sitting so close to it, you're going to go blind."

"A myth," I reply dismissively, trying to get him to shut up so I can hear this next bit, eyes fastened to the screen.

Artemis sighs, and above, I hear the creak and groan of floorboards, signaling that Tori is up in the sitting room pacing...again.

She doesn't show how much she's worried in front of me, but even if I couldn't see it hidden in her violet-hued stare—which I definitely *could*—I could also see it clear as the rising sun in the discoloration of her soul. Usually, it's a steady glow emanating from within her, but her worry has marred it. Made it spotty. Wavering. Pulsating with panic.

"Well, are you at least going to eat something today?"

I hold up a half-eaten box of stale crackers and shake it in answer. Then gesture the box toward the empty jar of spicy red pepper jelly I'd polished off for lunch earlier.

I don't need to look to see his eye roll. The kid had damn near perfected it in the last four days since Kincaid vanished and didn't return.

The shake of the cracker box made Kincaid's demonic cat lift its sleepy head from my lap, and I settle my hand on its spiny back, stroking gently to soothe it back to sleep.

The thing had grown on me in the past few days. Taking to sitting with me while I watched film after film, letting The Count of Monte Cristo, Titanic, Casper, and Independence Day push the hours forward. The other VHS tapes I dug out of a wilted box in the corner of the basement didn't seem to want to work no matter how many times I tried.

"I wish I never told you about the stupid TV," Artemis mutters under his breath. "Going to turn into a damned zombie."

A little bolt of fear races down my spine at his words, and I dip my head, trying to conceal the emotion from him. I doubt he's ever seen a zombie, but I have. Or at least, something close to that. The night at Bellefontaine cemetery. The night Kincaid made me curl my hand around that vile spirit scepter.

They'd tried to crawl from the earth. All bones and frayed, decaying flesh.

And the smell. I almost gag at the mere memory of it.

But zombified corpses weren't the only things we had the pleasure of meeting that night. There had been spirits, too. A few sad ones. A couple guilty. And one *very* pissed off lord of Hell. Kincaid's brother Malphas had appeared to me, begged me to tell his brother that he was dead. To warn him of what might happen to him, too.

Is that where Kincaid is then? In some other spirit plane? Dead?

Is that why he didn't come back to me like he promised he would?

The television isn't the only reason I tarry my days away in this cold dank cellar. I could just as easily have carried it upstairs. My strength has returned in spades since Tori dragged me back here from the Midnight Court. Strength, I can't help but notice, that is slightly *inhuman.*

But no, the reason I spend my minutes and hours and days here is because *they* can't get to me. Upstairs, I'm free game for the spirits to cajole and harass at all hours of the day and night. With my power only growing day by day, it's becoming increasingly difficult to shut them out. It requires too much energy.

Down here, though, the whispers are muted. Distant.

Whoever said basements are where the spooky things hang out have it all wrong. The old stone foundations here seem to create a sort of barrier that they can't cross.

As long as I stay here, I'm safe from them. As long as the TV stays on and at a decibel level somewhere above a normal volume and below blaring, I can get some peace.

Grumbling, I call to Artemis before he can leave. "Since you're here..."

Artemis turns, bare feet slapping the cool cement

floor as he makes his way over to the television and jabs the eject button on the ancient VCR. "Which one do you want?"

I ponder my very limited options, lips pursed. "Casper, I think. I've only watched that one twice now."

A soft sigh leaves his lips, and it's hard to miss how the aura of his spirit, usually a bright and cheery gold, dims just a little.

"You could watch it with me if you want?"

"Pass," he says as the screen flickers back to life and he steps aside.

The demonic cat on my lap nuzzles my hand for more pats, and I gasp, prompting Artemis to startle.

"What is it?" he says, face visibly paling as he takes in the air around us, wary that there may be malevolent spirits about.

"That's it!" I exclaim, lifting the cat so I can look him in his bright green eyes. "Casper. You may not be a friendly ghost, but you are a friendly demonic cat."

Artemis expels a disbelieving guffaw and a muttered, "*Yeah, right,*" keeping his distance. "That thing almost took Tori's eye out yesterday."

"Well, I still say it suits you," I say, lowering demon kitty until he's sitting upright on my lap, looking up at me curiously, head cocked. "You're as white as a ghost in any case."

"Didn't you say Kincaid told you not to name the cat?"

A sharp pang lances through me at the mention of

his name, and I work hard to conceal the pained expression trying to work its way onto my face. "No," I say carefully. "He said that Casper didn't *need* a name. Which is ridiculous. Everyone needs a name. Right, kitty?"

I give him a pat on his head. "Yours is Casper," I tell the cat, scratching him on his horned head. "Such a good boy, Casper."

He stiffens; his tail, that had been flicking back and forth a moment before, goes rigid. I wonder if he understands me.

"You don't like it?" I ask him, worried I've offended the thing.

Without warning he lifts himself on his hind legs and presses his paws to my chest, leaning in to lick my cheek. I giggle at first, but the sound quickly chokes off as a burning sensation spreads through my chest.

I take Casper's paws and lower him from my face.

"*Ugh,*" I mutter. "I think you're right, Art. I do need some real food. I think that jelly gave me heartburn."

A sharp pain in the side of my index finger makes me start, jumping to my feet and sending Casper to scuttle away, hissing at Artemis as he goes.

"He bit me…" I trail off, wiping the tiny droplets of blood onto my sweater. I stare incredulously after the cat, noticing something about him I hadn't before. A faint aura. The pale green of new leaves.

I squint to make certain it isn't a trick of the light, but Casper vanishes up the stairs before I can tell.

"Told you that thing wasn't safe."

I shake out the sting and push my messy hair back from my face, cringing at its greasy state. A good wash is quickly becoming a necessity instead of a luxury. I sigh, knowing it's time to brave the whispering voices upstairs, if only for the fifteen minutes it will take to scrub the days of hermitting off my skin and grab something more substantial to eat.

As I gather my trash from beside the weathered armchair, a familiar smell makes me pause. Sulfur. My eyes widen, and I whirl, finding Artemis staring at me with a brow raised, alarm in his eyes.

"Paige, what's wrong?"

I don't have to answer him. Not more than a second later, a thud sounds above us and then the shouting begins. Tori's voice rises above the sound of blood rushing in my ears.

"It's him," I say in a breath, hands shaking as I drop the empty cracker box and jar back to the cement floor, rushing past Artemis and into the stairwell.

I take the stairs two at a time, nearly tripping in my haste. Around the bend, down the corridor, and out into the front entryway.

There, hunched, with his skin steaming lightly in the center of the grand foyer, is Kincaid. The relief is staggering, and I have to catch myself on the gnarled wood of the banister to keep myself upright.

"You *asshole*." Tori is seething at him from where she stands in the doorway to the sitting room. She crosses the floor and shoves Kincaid in the chest. The first time, he lets her. The second time, he catches her arms.

His head lowers to stare into her violet eyes.

"Enough," he snarls and then releases her.

"Do you have any idea how long it's been? I thought you were dead."

She wasn't the only one.

Tori shakes her head, catching sight of me from the corner of her eye. She winces and I flush scarlet, wondering just how terrible I must look.

Kincaid turns, his yellow eyes reflecting a myriad of emotions. Grief. Frustration. Pain. But also, as his gaze meets mine, a flash of genuine relief.

Then his eyes flit away again and a hollowness burrows into my belly.

"You may leave," he says to Tori.

Tori just glares in response, her slender fingers clenching to fists at her sides until her knuckles blanche.

"Or you may stay. It matters not."

"Dick," she barks in reply, stomping to the coatrack to grab a jacket to throw over the clothes she borrowed from me. "*Thanks Tori. Oh, no problem Kincaid,*" she mocks in reply to herself. "My fucking pleasure."

She shoved her arms into the jacket and grits her teeth, and she sweeps the door open hard enough that it bounces against the opposite wall.

"I'll check in soon," she promises me, and I give her a nod.

"Thanks, Tori."

She side-eyes Kincaid one last time before departing, and I jump as the door clatters to a close.

Kincaid makes no move to leave the foyer, even after she's gone. He stands resolute, his gaze slowly roving the floor near his feet. I want to go to him, but something gives me pause.

Before his brother died in front of us…

Before I accidentally piggybacked on his ride to Hell…

He'd kissed me. And I'd be lying if I said that between nightmares of Ford and of all manner of terrible things happening to my lord of Hell, I didn't dream of him doing it again. And again and again.

My thighs clench, and I swallow hard, at war with my desire to go to him and my rational mind telling me that would be the last thing he wants. I am the one who proclaimed his brother to be dead. I brought scrutiny down on him by somehow miraculously surviving the trip to Hell and back.

At least, it seems there is no Diablim brave enough to come for me at Kincaid's house, but word on the street is they are watching for a chance to corner me.

I overheard Tori telling Artemis what her contacts passed on to her. It isn't good.

"Have you…" Kincaid trails off, and I watch as the inky blackness of his demon form begins to creep up his fingers, coating his knuckles, then his wrists, before he is able to stave it off. "Have you heard anything?"

I know what he means. He's asking if I've heard from Dantalion. Or perhaps anything else from Malphas. I bite my lower lip, dropping my head in shame as I rub a scuff out of the marble floor with my bare foot. "No. I'm sorry."

His lips press into a thin line, and he draws a breath through his nostrils, lifting a hand to pinch the bridge of his nose.

"Not even a whisper?"

I can't tell him I've been actively doing everything in my power *not* to hear any whispers at all. In fact, this is the first time I've been upstairs for more than a few minutes to use the bathroom in three days, and already I can hear them.

Not Dantalion or Malphas but the others. The indeterminate word sounds scratching at the inside of my skull, trying to find purchase in the divots and grooves there. Trying to burrow. To stay.

"No," I repeat, but watching how his face falls is like a rock on the windshield of my heart and the next words trip out of my mouth before I can stop them. "But if you want, I can try?"

He lifts his head again, eyes searching mine. It's so hard to hold his gaze. I'm worried he can see right through me. I know for a fact he can sense my emotions, and I work overtime to lock them down. He doesn't need to know I'm terrified he'll make me use the staff again. Or that I'd give anything to feel his arms around me.

He looks like a man on the edge. Utterly spent and staring down into an abyss that he knows there's no escaping.

"Don't fret, *Na'vazēm.* I'll not leave you again. It's no longer safe here without me."

A spike of ice penetrates my core at his words, but he's mistaken. He's reading my emotions all wrong. The fear I feel is not for my own safety. The worry creasing my brow isn't for myself at all.

I take in the tattered mess of his fine clothes, realizing with another twist in my gut that they are the same ones he wore that night at the Midnight Court. He hasn't changed. And judging by the darkness forming hollow pits beneath his eyes, he hasn't slept, either.

Trying to exude strength I do not feel, I don't hesitate as I step forward and tug his hand into mine.

Kincaid glances down at our twined fingers. He brushes a thumb over my knuckles, and I shiver.

"Come with me," I tell him, cursing the way my voice wavers.

Artemis hovers near the end of the hall, and I try to communicate with a sad smile that I'll be busy for a while. His eyes spark with a knowing gleam, and my smile turns sour. I roll my eyes at him. The little shit.

Kincaid lets me lead him upstairs. He doesn't protest as I push open the door to his bedroom and then shut it behind us. His room smells of him. Like hickory and warm musk.

To our left, a bed with tall wooden posts of the darkest mahogany languishes with a mess of silken sheets and thick blankets atop it. At the end of the bed is a wide, cushioned bench, and I tug him to it, gesturing for him to sit.

He falls onto it with a sigh and scrubs his wide palms over his face.

I kneel, busying my hands with the laces on his boots.

"What are you doing?" he asks, and I peer up to find him watching me.

"You need a bath. And rest."

He quirks a brow, and I try not to die of embarrassment when his gaze washes over my hair and the crumbs littering the front of my wool sweater. He says nothing, though, and I'm able to pluck what's left of my dignity from the floor.

I remove his boots and socks before standing to push his jacket from his shoulders and then unbutton his dress shirt. My fingers fumble on the third button from the top as a smooth expanse of golden chest is revealed beneath.

I curse at myself internally, almost ready to give up when Kincaid closes his hand around my clumsy ones and removes them from his torn and soot-streaked shirt. I drop them to my lap and a ball forms in my throat.

Hell-warmed fingers press gently against the

bottom of my chin until we're at eye-level with one another.

"I didn't think you were coming back," I blurt before I can help myself and condemn the tears stinging in the corners of my eyes.

Without a word, he releases my face and I'm in his arms. He pulls me tightly to his chest, and I grip the remains of fabric still clinging to his skin, burying my wet cheeks into him as his hand moves to grip the back of my neck, holding me in place against him. Somehow, I've ended up on his lap, and I have no idea how it happened. I hold him tightly, hating that I need this.

That I need him.

"We must talk," he whispers against the mess of my hair, and I pull back, self-conscious as I climb from his lap and swipe at my cheeks.

"Y-you should bathe first. And sleep."

He cocks his head at me and a dangerous glint passes over his eyes, reminding me exactly who I'm talking to. Asmodeus. One of the seven lords of Hell. No matter the connection I feel between us—that I think he feels too—nothing will change who and what he is.

Dangerous. A *demon*.

"If anyone will be bathing this evening, it's you," he says, and the playful edge to the words takes some of my doubt away.

"But I'm afraid this cannot wait *Na'vazēm*. "You're in danger."

2

"And you're not?" I scoff. "I'm no detective, but I'm fairly certain not one but two lords of Hell, *unkillable* lords of Hell, are dead."

Guilt punches me in the gut just as swiftly as the reminder of his grief hits him, but I will not apologize.

"You've been gone for days, and I'm still here. Unharmed."

His upper lip curls back, and I fall back a step, seeing the threat in the way his hands darken with the blackness of his demon once more.

"Must you be so insufferable, woman?"

"Must you be so damned cliche?"

"Cliche?"

I throw my hands up. "You're more worried about my safety when yours is clearly—"

"Stop." He holds up a hand in warning, and I

remember my place, clenching my teeth against a biting retort.

"I'll not argue with you. I don't have the patience."

"Fine." We could figure out what to do later. His brain is clearly fried. "I'll run you a bath."

I turn to cross the room, assuming there's a bathroom hiding in the shadows beyond an open door at the other end of Kincaid's chamber.

He snatches my wrist before I can move, though, jerking me to a standstill.

"We can talk later, but we *will* talk. There is much you need to know. Much we have to do."

Grimly, I nod.

"Na'vazēm, you are not to leave this house without me. Not even for a second. Do you understand?"

"Is that an order?"

"Yes."

I jerk my hand free of his grasp and walk away without answering.

"Paige," he all but snarls and I halt, shoulders rising as a shiver snakes down my spine. And I must be even more messed up than I thought I was because something in his threatening tone excites me.

"Do you understand?" he repeats.

"Yes, Kincaid," I reply in a flat monotone before finding the light switch in the bathroom and closing myself inside for some privacy as I catch my breath, falling back against the smooth grain of the door.

I tip my head back and breathe deeply to steady

myself. As terrifying as Kincaid can be when he wants to, something inside of me knows that he won't hurt me. At least not on purpose. Not like Ford did.

And maybe that's naive. You know what, it probably is, but I don't care. I want to believe it.

I want to believe it more than I've ever wanted to believe anything in my entire miserable existence.

Move, Paige, I tell myself, shoving off from the door to face a wide tiled space with a long porcelain tub crouching at its center. It bows in the middle and is easily the largest I've ever seen.

A glass-encased shower stands to one side of the space, and a partition wall hugs around what I assume is a toilet, while a bank of two sinks lies against the wall straight across from me and behind the tub. With raised bowls that look as though they're made of solid gold.

I kneel as I turn the faucets on, adjusting the hot and cold as I go. Disappointingly, the rush of water gushing from the spigots does little to dull the burgeoning roar of whispers in my head. They get stronger with each passing minute, and I have to work hard to block them, giving myself a headache in the process.

I distract myself with random thoughts, wondering if the water should be hotter since it's meant to bathe a demon. I mean, he's used to the heat of Hell. Perhaps he likes his bathwater scalding. Perhaps he doesn't bathe at all.

The tap handles are a little stuck and I need to rinse a fine layer of dust from the belly of the tub before I'm even able to begin filling it.

Nervous flutters converge in my belly as I hear the click and groan of the door opening at my back and feel Kincaid's presence as he enters. I feel the water again as the bath edges closer to full, deciding that it does in fact need to be hotter. I turn down the cold tap and gulp, feeling all kinds of uncomfortable.

In my peripherals, I see the shirt I'd been working to remove from Kincaid fall to the floor in a heap, followed swiftly by his pants. The metal buckle of his belt clatters against the cool tile and my mouth goes dry.

Time to go.

I shut off the faucets and get shakily to my feet.

"I'll see you in the morning?"

I meant for it to be a statement, and yet it leaves my lips as a question. A pleading one at that. I need to hear him say he'll be here when I wake up, or I'm not sure I'll be able to sleep at all.

Hell, sleep may be out of the question regardless at this point.

"In the morning?" His rich voice fills the space, expanding through the room until I can feel the press of it like warm breath on my cheek. "No, *Na'vazēm.* I'll not have you leave my side. Not tonight."

I stiffen, wanting so badly to fight him. To tell him I won't stay.

But the truth is: I want to.

"Come. Bathe."

My head snaps up, lips parting as I take in Kincaid's body. He stands without a scrap of clothing to cover him and dips two fingers into the bathwater, a small groan of pleasure rumbling in his chest that does all kinds of things to my nerves.

His yellow eyes cut to me for an instant, and a little smirk lifts the corner of his mouth. I wonder how I must look, gaping at him, completely unable to stop staring at his cock and the powerful lines of his body. I've never seen a man naked, at least never more than illustrations in textbooks or romantic movie scenes.

"I nearly forgot," he says offhandedly, sliding himself into the water with a sigh.

"Forgot what?"

"How prude mortals are."

And I'd nearly forgotten how demons and demonkind seemed to have not so much as an ounce of modesty.

"I'm not mortal," I reply, taking his comment for what it is. A challenge.

I strip down to my panties before pausing, finding myself unable to remove the final garment despite the bravery of a second before. My nipples pebble at the rush of cool air as I discard my sweater and tank top, stepping into the tub with a hiss at the temperature.

Kincaid stares at the double sinks as I sink below the water-level, nearly causing it to slosh out of the sides. I'd accounted for one body to be submerged, but not two.

I blush as my breasts bob in the water, and he turns back to face me, the minute of considerate privacy he gave me spent.

His hungry gaze roams over my face and down to the mounds of my breasts, but no lower.

A scared little voice in my head shouts, *"now what,"* over the din of incoherent whispers battling in the background.

My legs brush against and tangle with Kincaid's. The soft, slippery feeling of our wet bodies against one another almost undoes me, and I have to sink a little lower into the water and tip my head back to keep myself sane.

A soft growl emanates from where he sits opposite me, arms lazily splayed against the edges of the tub. "Control yourself, *Na'vazēm,* or I cannot promise to stop myself."

I level a heated stare on his lips. "And if I don't want you to stop yourself?"

He bares his teeth and lurches forward, startling me as his hands slip up to my forearms, effortlessly spinning me in the water until my back is pressed against his and I can feel the bulge of his erection against my lower back.

"Be still," he commands, and aside from the raucous beating of my heart and the quick rise and fall of my chest, I do as I'm told, my hands clenched to a bruising tightness against my belly.

He releases me, and I hear the pop of a cap and turn to see him draw up a bottle from the side of the tub that'd been concealed from me when I walked in.

"I said be still," he reaffirms.

I start as he presses gently down on my shoulders, tipping my chin back so my hair is beneath the water and my face is bared to him. His eyes trace the lines of my lips as he strokes his fingers through my hair quickly and then helps me back up.

He lathers a rich shampoo through my hair, using the tips of his fingers to massage my scalp as he goes. I lean into him despite his command to remain still and this time he doesn't berate me. When he's finished, he rinses it out and repeats the process with conditioner.

Showing more patience than I thought him capable of.

Something in my expression as he rinses the spice-scented conditioner from my hair makes him pause, and I open my eyes to find a crease between his brows. With my ears beneath the water, the voices in my head strengthen, making it even more difficult to tune them out.

"What is it?" Kincaid asks as I lift my head.

I squint my eyes against the ever-growing ache behind my eye- cavities and shake my head. "It's nothing. Just...the voices. They're getting harder to block."

"Is it..."

"No. I don't hear them."

To be fair, I wasn't trying to, but if Dantalion or Malphas are somehow in this room with us right now, while I'm naked between their brother's legs in a bathtub, I think I'd rather not know.

"You stupid bitch!"

One of the voices breaks off from the whole, gaining clarity. I shove it back, but it only surges forward again.

"Let me in," it cries, and my blood goes cold as I fight off the sensation of icy fingers clawing at my skull. Of a foreign presence filling a gap I didn't know existed.

"Paige?"

"Can they get in?" I ask in a rush, whirling to face him. "Can they possess me?"

His angular jaw goes slack at my question, and it's the only answer I need.

"Hold on." He grunts, disentangling himself from me as he lifts from the water, uncaring that he's soaking the floor as he flings a towel around his waist and lurches out the door.

"Let me in!" the voice in my head shouts, and I grit my teeth, gripping my head between my palms.

"No." I groan. *"Get out."*

Vaguely, I remember something in the book on Necromancy that Kincaid gave me to read about this, but the memory is distant, and I can't reach it. I haven't looked at that book since we returned from the Midnight Court. Like an idiot, I sat and waited in the dank cold of the basement for Kincaid to return instead of doing anything useful.

"Here." Kincaid's return alarms me enough that water sloshes out of the tub again when I jump. He tugs my right hand from my temple, and I feel the cool rub of beads as he tugs them onto my wrist.

I try to recoil, but he holds fast, forcing bracelet after bracelet onto my wrist until all the bracelets Ford gave me are back on. I want to barf at the very sight of them.

But...the voices...

I stop struggling, letting my hand rest in his as he hunches next to the tub. "How?"

I can still hear them, but it's almost as if I'm back in the basement. Embraced by stone and mortar. In the back of my head, they buzz like a swarm of wasps around a hive. But they can't get in. They are firmly *outside*.

My shoulders slump, and I lie back against the tub, my hand slipping from Kincaid's.

"How did you know?"

"I noticed them the first time I saw you. Peculiar that a mortal should be wearing shadow beads when the only place that particular stone can be found is in Hell."

I lift my arm from the water, staring at the tiny smooth gems with new eyes.

"I wasn't certain that's what they were, but I am now."

I always thought they were peculiar. The texts I had on gemstones didn't show any quite like these. Obsidian black but with a multitude of colors hidden beneath if viewed in the correct light.

"They block spiritual attack," Kincaid explains. "Against a very strong spirit, I doubt they would be enough, but it seems for now, they are."

"Ford knew exactly what I was," I mutter, the words more for myself than for him. A deep ache forms in my chest. "He knew, and he tried to condition me against it. Like he thought if he just—"

I can't continue as my hands ball to fists and an entirely different kind of tears burn in my eyes.

"You're right." Kincaid snaps me out of my rage with his curious tone. "He knew."

He stands, wiping a hand over the stubble on his jaw. "He might know something more. Have some clue as to your origin."

"He's dead," I remind Kincaid, realizing a little belatedly what he's implying. "*No.*"

Kincaid's eyes narrow.

"I am not going to speak to his spirit. You can't make me."

I stand in a rush, almost slipping in my haste to get out of the tub, still feeling the phantom press of his stare. "I won't do it, Kincaid."

"Very well," he replies, crossing his arms over his chest as I rip a towel from a neat stack, sending the rest of them careening to the floor. Hands trembling, I bend to pick them up, fire in my cheeks.

Kincaid stops me with a hand pressed to my back. I flinch away from his touch and scowl, unable to meet his eyes.

"Then perhaps there may be some clue to help us at your home."

"That place is not my home," I snap back, pulling the towel tight around my body.

Kincaid's brows lower, and he steps away, contemplative. "Will you accompany me, or shall I go alone? I wager it'll be easier to search the house with you there to guide me."

"But it's across The Hinge."

"I did vow to get you across once our bargain is complete. There is a way across. It is not over the river but under it."

I cock my head at him, picturing a cold, damp tunnel beneath the earth. My pulse quickens as I consider his request. I swore to myself I'd never go back there, but I didn't have to go to the dead room. I wouldn't have to go into the room with the chair, or the one with the drain in the floor. I'd just have to guide him through the house. I could fetch some of my things.

My weighted blanket!

For that alone, I'd go.

"Okay," I murmur.

Brushing my damp hair back from my face, I bite

my lip. "But I still think figuring out exactly what or who is responsible for killing lords of the underworld is much more important than—"

His face darkens.

"I've already looked," he interrupts.

I open my mouth to argue, but the look he's giving me makes whatever I'd been about to say desiccate on my lips.

"My brothers began to vanish after you arrived in Elisium," he says, and I don't correct him. They haven't vanished. They are dead. "I think it's possible the two events are somehow tied."

"You don't think I have anything to do with—"

"If I did, you would be dead."

Noted.

"What if you're wrong? What if my arrival here has absolutely nothing to do with the other lords and we're just wasting time?"

A muscle in his jaw ticks. "Then I will be dead. And you will be free."

3

I was right. I can't sleep.

I toss and turn in Kincaid's bed. It's much larger than mine, and the fact that it's empty of him both comforts and frustrates me. What he said just before tossing me a tunic of his to wear to sleep carved out a nook in my head, and I can't be rid of it.

Then I will be dead and you will be free.

Would I?

Did I want to be?

Would I survive if he did not?

The questions surrounding that single sentence drove me to the edge of insanity. Freedom from captivity was all I'd ever wanted, since I'd consciously begun to understand what captivity was and that I was a slave to it.

I groaned, turning back onto my side and forcing

my eyes shut as I punched the corner of the pillow into shape.

"Are you always this disturbed in sleep, *Na'vazēm?*"

"Only when forced to share a room with a demon," I sling back bitterly.

A chuckle in the dark only serves to further heat the blood already boiling in my veins.

"Glad you think it's so funny."

There's a shift in the shadows, and I squint, easily able to make my Diablim eyes adjust to the dark. Kincaid stands from his makeshift bed on the floor and tips his head to one side, cracking his neck. "If we are to lie awake until dawn, I'd prefer to do it in my own bed."

I shuffle over to make room for him, a prickle of anticipation raising the hairs on my arms and tightening something low in my belly. "I didn't ask you to sleep on the floor."

"I should flog you for the way you speak to me."

Did he just say...*flog?* Did people even say that anymore?

I'm aware that I'm overtired, underfed, and—let's face it—hot for a demon I should hate. That was enough of an excuse to have a shitty attitude, wasn't it?

Kincaid's body heat slithers beneath the covers with him, and I shiver, my new side of the bed icy cold by comparison. "Shall we talk now, since it seems neither of us can sleep?"

"Shoot."

I can hear his smile in the dark.

"You caused quite the stir in Elisium. Word of your ability has reached as far as Aetherium on Earth, and is beginning to spread through the underworld. No doubt the angels are just as curious as the damned."

"And?"

"And you need to know the threat that poses. Only the seven lords can come and go from Hell and live. Not even Lucifer himself has that luxury."

"And why is that?"

"We keep order," Kincaid explains. "Each of us—the lords—commands one of the seven Fallen Cities. The staff I use to travel back and forth was a gift."

"A gift?" I prod.

"From the archangel Gabriel." He snorts. "As if I would want to return to Hell. We keep order in the cities. If we fail to do so…there will be open war between Heaven and Hell on earth. That is something neither side wishes to happen."

"So, the cities that Dantalion and Malphas oversaw…?"

"We're taking care of it. That isn't the point."

"Then what is?"

Kincaid pinches the bridge of his nose. "The point is that you should not have the ability to travel between this plane and the other. It's not possible."

Seems to be the story of my life. Making the impossible possible.

Impossible that I could be Diablim, and yet I am.

Impossible that I should have been able to cross The Hinge, and yet I did.

Impossible that I could hear and see the spirits of Kincaid's fallen demon brothers, and yet I had.

Now it seems I can travel to Hell and back, a right only reserved for seven demons—also somehow extended to me.

"There are many who will wish to unravel you now, *Na'vazēm*. In more ways than one."

I clutched the covers tighter around myself, drawing my legs up to try to get some warmth into my cold toes.

"The Carver , it seems, has taken a keen interest."

"The...Carver?"

"You are *abnormal,*" Kincaid replies, ignoring my query. "And those aren't tolerated on any plane of existence. For now, you're simply a curiosity. I need to keep it that way."

Even I know what they say about that. Except in my case I don't think curiosity will kill the curious. Me, however, it just might.

"What is going to happen to me?"

I hate how my voice sounds small and high, like a child's. I dig my fingernails into my knees, remembering who I am. Remembering everything I've survived. And I feel better.

I can't be broken so easily. My limits have been tested.

Warm hands seize me beneath the covers, bring me

close until the length of him is pressed against the length of me. I press my cold nose into his neck, and he flinches.

"You are *mine*," he hisses. "If one so much as touches you, they will lose the offending hand."

I want to believe him, but where his chin rests at the precipice of my skull, I feel a twitch. His arms around me tighten as though he truly is afraid to let me out of his sight for even a second.

"Sleep now," Kincaid commands, and I feel the heated flood of his power seep into my skin. It delves deep into muscle and sinew. Excavates the disquieting thoughts from my mind and leaves nothing behind but a comforting dark.

I sigh against him, falling into the void.

4

I'm ravenous.

My belly burbles and grumbles as I fetch a plate of Tori's macaroni and cheese from the casserole dish in the fridge.

At least one of us knew how to actually cook for a while in the house. I hadn't the stomach to eat much of anything while Kincaid was gone, but now I heft three large scoops of the congealed cheese and noodles onto my plate, not even bothering to warm it up first before snatching up a fork and heading to the dining room.

Kincaid slept deeply when I finally woke sometime in the early afternoon. He hadn't so much as stirred as I rose from the bed. His face had been buried in a pillow so I couldn't see his expression, but the softness of his body in slumber made me want to trail fingers over the wide expanse of his bare back. Or brush my fingers through his raven black hair.

How could something so lethal look so *ethereal* in sleep?

Something Pattywort told me about him returns, and I wonder at the truth of it. If Kincaid truly was once an angel. If he'd fallen from grace.

"Sleep well?" Artemis asks as I enter the dining room, nearly making me topple the entire plate of mac and cheese in surprise. I'm glad I had a mind to get dressed in my room before coming down.

His smirk tells me he knew exactly what he was doing, and I shoot him a glare.

"Fine," I reply, dragging a chair noisily from the table to sit down opposite him at the long dark wood table.

Artemis stuffs his face with a bite of Lucky Charms and chews with his mouth open as he grins. His eyebrows waggling. "Better than fine, I bet."

"Remind me again why I tried to save you?"

Art shrugs, flipping his muddy brown hair out of his face as he takes another bite. Milk drips from his chin as he replies, "Beats me."

"Ugh," I gag, giving him a very pronounced eye roll to which he just grins more. I take back every time in my life I ever wished I had a sibling to share in my misery. It is *not* how I imagined it would be.

Besides, I wouldn't have subjected anyone to the childhood I'd had to endure.

"Oh!" I gasp as Casper leaps up onto my lap under the table and curls up, purring animatedly against my stomach. "Have you forgiven me now?" I ask, sinking the fingers of my left hand into his fur while the right busies itself with a cold breakfast.

As if in answer, Casper pushes his nose against my knuckles and rubs his little face over the side of my hand. I don't know why I ever thought he was so scary. "That's a good boy," I croon, sitting back to get a look at him.

I cock my head, finding the aura I'd thought I'd seen around him in the basement yesterday wasn't a trick of the light after all. *Hmm.*

His green eyes open along with his mouth, showing a little row of nubby teeth sandwiched between his itty-bitty fangs. The eyes are what draw me, though. Brighter than ever before.

My power must still be strengthening if I can see a demon cat's spirit aura so easily now when there had been virtually nothing there before.

"Can I ask you something without you giving me a smartass response?" I question after a time of eating in relative silence, with only Casper's purring and the scrape of cutlery on china for sound.

Artemis purses his lips, as though what I'm asking of him is some great feat that he isn't certain he can accomplish.

"*Artemis*," I grouse, dropping my fork back to my plate.

"All right, fine. What?"

I straighten in my seat, trying to appear casual. "Do you know of someone called the Carver?"

Artemis' hand stills barely an inch from his lips. His bright brown eyes consider me carefully. "Why?"

"Are you nearly ready to leave?" Kincaid enters from the library, and both our heads swivel in his direction. He shoots a warning glance at Artemis, and I know for certain now that I'll never find out who the hell the Carver is.

Art resumes eating double-time, polishing off the remains of his massive cereal bowl so he can leave.

I shove my plate away. "I guess so."

"Where are you going?" Artemis asks and then winces, casting an apologetic glance Kincaid's way. I'm reminded of where he'd been before he came here and wonder how many ruthless hands he's been passed through and for how long.

That he feels regret and fear at asking a simple question in the presence of his master tells me it's likely been his whole life. The same as me.

"To where I lived before. To look for clues of what I am. Where I came from."

"To the mortal side of the river?"

"*Paige*," Kincaid warns, and I realize he doesn't trust Artemis knowing where we're going. Which is ridiculous. He lives in this house. He'll find out one way or another. And besides, I trust him.

Comforting myself by stroking Casper's soft fur, I give Artemis a nod.

Kincaid washes a hand over his face and gives me an appraising look. "You do realize that I'll have to kill him now?"

"If you mean because I'm not supposed to know about the Underbridge, I already do. That's how I was smuggled into Elisium."

"And you didn't go running to tell the first Nephilim you saw?"

"Why? I don't have a death wish."

Kincaid makes a noncommittal sound and eyes Artemis in a way that has me on my toes beneath the table, ready to shove Casper from my lap and leap between them if I have to.

"You may join us," he finally decides, and I melt back into the wooden chairback. "But you will tell me who smuggled you across."

There brokers no room for argument in Kincaid's tone and Artemis' mouth snaps shut. A real and vivid fear brightens his eyes, almost as brightly as his pulsating aura. Wild and undulating with terror. Turning a sickly shade of grayish green.

"Kincaid," I say in a soft tone, trying to reason with him, but he hushes me sharply.

"I'm afraid this type of betrayal must be dealt with. Only a very small few Diablim in Elisium know of the Underbridge and even fewer have access to it. Brining a Nephilim, *or anyone,* through those tunnels is expressly prohibited."

"Will he know it was me who told you?"

Kincaid considers this for a moment before replying. "Yes."

Artemis shudders, and it's almost too much for me to take. I give Kincaid an imploring look until he relents.

"But there won't be time for the offender to tell another soul before his is swiftly taken."

It took me far too long to catch on that we were calmly talking about murder here. Or more aptly, an execution.

Artemis' throat bobbed before he replied, "Zak."

Kincaid didn't show even a lick of surprise. Not a hint of anger.

He *smiled.*

"Finish up. We leave in ten minutes."

I pushed my chair back and scooched demon kitty from my lap, "Go on, Casper. We'll be back soon."

Kincaid startles, and a low growl pulls my attention from Casper to him, frozen in the doorway. His horns jut out from his skull, curving up and out as his hands turn black, a stark contrast to the white tunic he wears.

"Casper?" he demands, eyes glowing brightest gold in a face quickly being consumed by darkness. The fabric of his jeans and tunic strain against his demon form, and despite myself, I cower, nearly knocking the chair over as I back away.

Artemis has backed up, too, and together we both stand against the old buffet and hutch where Kincaid's spirits permeate the air with a cloying sweetness.

"I—you...you said it didn't have a name so—"

"You *named* it?"

"It needed a name! I don't know why you're being such a dick about it."

Kincaid laughs darkly, and it's worse than if he'd shouted, but at least some of the darkness of his demon form is receding. My pulse slows, and I lengthen my spine, trying not to show just how much he scared me.

He mutters something in another language beneath his breath, and I don't have to speak it myself to know that it's something rude. Probably laden with a truck-load of curses.

When his demon form has all but vanished completely, leaving him in some freshly stretched clothes, he closes his eyes. "We'll deal with this later."

Deal with what, I want to ask, but I can tell now is not the time to press him. He leaves, still fuming and chuckling—a terrifying combination that has me worried I've done something very, *very* wrong.

"I told you not to name it," Artemis says in a low voice, and I elbow him in the ribs, growling.

"Shut up."

5

"It's here?"

They're the first two words I've spoken to Kincaid since we left the house, deciding that I'd slide into the backseat with Artemis, forcing Kincaid to take the front or else be squished in with us.

The Midnight Court looks nothing like it did under the light of the full moon. In the pale light of a cloudy day, it just looks like any other fancy building. An abandoned one at that. With only one stationary host standing sentinel at the entrance when the driver pulls up.

Now there is only a stone pathway and immaculately cared for shrubbery and freshly trimmed grass.

"My lord." The host bows as we pass, and Kincaid doesn't spare him so much as a glance.

Our footsteps echo in the entry, and unable to help myself, I peer into the grand ballrooms, finding them speckless and devoid of life. The floors polished to a mirror shine, reflecting strange murals on the ceiling I hadn't noticed the last time.

At least we're alone. I'd wrung my hands to the point they felt chapped on the way here, wondering which boogeyman would be the one to make a move for me. To pick me apart and find what makes me tick.

But it seemed, so far at least, that Kincaid is right. So long as he's with me, or I'm within the walls of his home, I am safe.

It's a small comfort. If only I could offer him the same protection.

"Na'vazēm!"

I rush to catch up, a stone weight in my belly when I see where he's leading us. Around the main entry and down a flight of stairs to a cold stone pathway. We pass the exact spot where he pressed me up against the wall and...

Our eyes meet in the dark for an instant before I break the contact, gaze firmly back on the ground.

The door to the gambling floor opens and a rush of sound drenches my senses along with a metallic odor. Like sweat mixed with strong liquor.

We enter into another world, entirely divergent from the quiet streets outside. Down here, a realm of sin throbs as though contained in a beating heart. Music thuds behind my breastbone and bodies crush together. Naked Diablim dance around shining silver poles, and a group of horned men shout and cajole one another around a card table.

Slot machines whir and *ping,* eliciting sounds of glee and disappointment all around.

Artemis doesn't seem at all enthralled or interested in the place, preferring to keep his head down and eyes front. Perhaps I should've done the same. We don't get more than several paces in before I begin to notice the heads turning, devilish eyes calculating. Searching.

Curious.

I nearly run into Kincaid when he stops abruptly and leans in to say something to a Diablim man in a black tuxedo wearing an earpiece. The man nods and then speaks into the watch on his wrist, relaying an order I do not hear.

He then waves Kincaid through a doorway in the wall that you would never know was there if someone didn't tell you.

The sounds and smells and heat of the gambling floor evaporate as the door shuts behind us.

"This way," Kincaid says in a dead monotone, and I keep on his heels, not wanting to get lost as the long corridor forks off into several smaller ones. Kincaid scans his palm on not one but *three* different doorways as we delve deeper down and farther in.

It's just after the third door where he pauses, his breath lightly clouding the air in front of his face, making my sudden desire for a jacket seem all the more warranted.

Tilting my head and listening carefully, I find that I can hear the river. I have no idea how far above us it runs, but there's a dull roar that for once is *not* the sound of spirits chattering incessantly in my head.

The compounding weight of all that water and earth over our heads is enough to make me curl in on myself.

"Is it just me or is it hard to breathe down here?"

Sweat drops down Artemis' head when he shakes it. "It's not just you. It sucks down here."

"If at any point you cannot bear the pain, we can turn back," Kincaid says, not bothering to turn around when he speaks. "This passage allows us to get across *alive,* but it doesn't come without a cost."

I sigh. I'm no stranger to pain but that doesn't mean I welcome it. "You could have warned me," I mutter before stepping past him, eager to get it over with. Staring down the barrel of a gun never helped anyone.

I lengthen my strides, taking long lungfuls of air in preparation for the pain. It comes swiftly, like walking through a forest of knives or over a carpet of poisonous spores. My vision wavers, and about halfway there I find I have no choice but to slow. I can't push myself on at the speed I'd maintained for the first half.

A vein in my forehead throbs in tune with my pulse, and I carve deep half-moons into my palms.

"You're doing great," Artemis whispers from beside me, and I feel the press of his fingers on my elbow, helping me along and also healing whatever damage the crossing is doing to my body.

I want to cry at the relief, but only a whimper gets past my teeth.

"So how old were you?" I ask, trying to distract myself.

"I was four when Zak took me."

I try to think of something else to ask, but I don't want to pry, and I can tell he doesn't relish remembering his past any more than I do. So I'm surprised when he continues on his own.

"It was to pay a debt." He turns his head back, and I think he must be looking at Kincaid lagging behind us. I can't hear him save for his footfalls, slow and measured. I hope he's all right.

"To Kincaid?" I wonder.

"To the casino, so, yes, I guess so. He kept me for about a week before he sold me at the Demon Market. I've passed hands three times since then."

I grunt, and Artemis wraps an arm around my lower back like a band, pushing his healing magic into me as he hurries me the rest of the way across. I lurch to my knees when the pain releases me, bending at the waist to vomit over the concrete.

Kincaid is there in a flash, lifting me from the damp disgust of the ground and into his arms.

"Thank you," I manage, swiping my sleeve over my lips.

Kincaid cocks his head.

"Not you. Him."

"Anytime." Artemis grins, and my heart warms and breaks all at once. Because I know that no matter what it takes, I won't allow Kincaid to bring him back to Elisium with us.

There has to be something I can say to convince him. A new bargain that can be struck.

Artemis will have his freedom. "It's not what I imagined," Artemis says with a sour look as the house comes into view.

"What were you imagining?" I ask, hating how my voice sounds strained even to my own ears.

Artemis bumps my shoulder. "Spires? Maybe a fire-breathing dragon? I don't know. Something *not* like this."

"Where did you live before? Are your parents—"

"Dead," he supplies without preamble. "Zak killed them before he took me."

The way he says it, so matter-of-factly, makes my blood boil. I kind of want to meet Zak so I can rip his black heart from his chest and then eat his soul for lunch. I'm a necromancer, maybe that's something I can do. I make a mental note to ask Kincaid.

My heart sputters as the car Kincaid stole from a parking garage rolls to a stop and I reach forward, gripping the back of the driver's seat tightly. "Something's wrong," I breathe. "The door's open."

The door is *never* open.

I swallow air as Kincaid steps out, scanning the desolate front lawn and the skies above us.

Ford is dead.

I have to actively remind myself as I shoulder open my own door, shivering despite the humid afternoon air. *He's dead. It's probably just squatters.*

But regardless of what I try to tell myself, I'm already picturing him. Picturing his shadowed brown eyes snapping open on that metal table. Picturing his bloated green-hued body reanimating as he lurches his way back to the house, waiting for me to return.

Ford is dead.

"There's no one here, *Na'vazēm.*"

I heave air into my lungs and shake out the sting in my fingertips as Artemis and I follow Kincaid inside. It's impossible not to remember the last time I stood at this door. When the officers told me Ford was dead.

The taste of freedom was fresh on my lips; I'd been eager to take a bite.

I'd been a fool.

Kincaid pushes the door the rest of the way open and steps into the entry, taking in the long hall and the panel in the wall. Littered over the floor are mottled leaves and small patches of dirt. There's enough light inside from the shatterproof windows that there's no need to turn on the lights. Good thing, too, because the hum of electricity is entirely absent in the house.

It's clearly been shut off.

Kincaid's demon form creeps up his forearms in

front of us where he's paused near Ford's bedroom door. It, too, is open.

It's strange, but seeing it that way. Ajar, with light from the windows inside painting a rectangular patch of light onto the hall floor, solidifies the fact he's dead.

That door only opened for him to pass through. Once in the morning. Once in the evening. I've never seen more than a glimpse of what lies within.

Artemis turns back to me as he passes to join Kincaid, "You coming?"

I'm not sure I can speak so I only nod, my face warming, though I'm not entirely sure why.

Artemis's mouth falls open when he peers into the room, and between Kincaid and him, I worry I don't want to see inside at all. Contemplate why in the world I ever did.

There is very likely all manner of awful things inside. I imagine a collection of cattle prods. Detailed blueprints of how to inflict the most pain on a human being—or rather—a Diablim.

So when my feet finally find purchase on the gritty floor, propelling me forward, I'm shocked to find nothing of the sort beyond the door.

It's a room just like any other. Or it would have been, before whatever came through it tore the entire space apart. A mattress and soot gray bedding lie at an odd angle atop a metal frame. Nightstand drawers jut open, their bowels spilled over the floor.

Likewise, a tall dresser has been ransacked. Clothes

spill from three of the remaining drawers while the others lie on the carpet, upturned or empty.

The whole place smells faintly of him, and with the taste of vomit still in my throat, I'm shocked I don't cough up whatever remains in my stomach. The glint of sunlight on glass catches my eye as I waver in place, a bout of vertigo threatening to take me.

It's a photograph. It lies faceup on the carpet near the edge of the shifted mattress. A crack in the glass. I clench my fists and enter the room, unwilling to allow myself to be frightened of a dead man's room.

The dead man himself, well, that's another story. But I don't feel his presence here. His voice isn't among the others humming at the edges of my consciousness.

I pick the broken glass from the worn wooden frame and toss it to the floor, squinting at the image. A woman with long dark hair and pretty green eyes stares back up at me. She has skin the color of clouded honey and a smile that beckons.

I trace the line of her jaw, and my throat thickens.

It's my mother.

I'm not sure how I know. Maybe it's the likeness of the shape of her face. Or the rounded tip of her slight nose. The curve of her long neck. They are all features I've seen in the mirror. She can't be more than twenty-five in this picture, and I am almost the spit of her.

"She was human," I find myself whispering, trying to convince myself. I never had reason to doubt it until recently, but this has to be proof, right? The woman in this photograph can't be Diablim.

"Who did this?" Artemis asks in a soft whisper, lifting the edge of a blanket to see what's underneath.

"Angels," Kincaid growls. "Their scent is on everything. They haven't been gone long."

Angels?

"*Damn,*" Kincaid hisses, throwing out an arm and sending the remains of the dresser smashing into the opposite wall. Wooden splinters explode onto the carpet, and I have to side-step to avoid getting hit.

"Is this bad? Why are the angels searching Ford's house?"

"The same reason we are," Kincaid replies, the words whistling through his clenched teeth. He runs a hand through his tousled black hair, muttering to himself. "I thought we had more time."

"They might have missed something," Artemis says, ever the optimist. He begins searching the closet near the splintered dresser and his fervor is contagious. Kincaid begins to search as well, going through the discarded things on the floor and ripping the backings from the bland artwork on the walls.

I gently wiggle the photo from the frame and fold it, tucking it into my back pocket, beginning to doubt as I watch Kincaid sift through Ford's things. When he isn't in his demon form, Kincaid could look almost mortal save for his eyes. Not just the strange ochre color of them, but the depth. The boundlessness of a millennium of life is captured in the flecks and waving lines of his irises. Like the rings hidden in a tree's trunk.

One look into his eyes and even a fool would know he's anything but human.

My mother could have been a demon. Or maybe Nephilim, I consider, lifting my gaze to the determined face of Artemis. Nephilim seems more likely, but that's a biased opinion based solely on her genuine smile in the photo.

"There's nothing in here," Kincaid grouses, stalking back to the door. "I'm going to search the rest of the house."

"Just a second," I call after him, glancing uneasily between him and Artemis. The entire car ride here my thoughts were preoccupied with how to ask Kincaid to release Artemis in just the right way that he would have to say yes. But now that I've finally gotten the gall to actually do it, all of the words I carefully planned out and laced together vanish from my mind as though they were never there at all.

Kincaid studies me, waiting with an impatient tick in his brow.

Off to a great start already.

"I was thinking," I start. "You really don't need two wards to worry about back in Elisium."

Artemis pales.

"Maybe…I mean maybe we could leave Artemis here. Where he belongs?"

Kincaid's nostrils flare.

"I'd be willing to barter for his freedom if that's what it takes."

I have no idea what I can offer him that he doesn't already have a right to. But an idea strikes a moment later, and I jump at it even though every nerve ending in my body is screaming at me not to do it.

"I'll hold the Spirit Scepter again," I blurt. "I can try to communicate with your brothers."

He was going to make me do it anyway, I was sure, but this way he would know that I wouldn't fight him on it.

Kincaid's lips pressed into a tight line. "No, *Na'vazēm.* I'll not barter for a thing I already own the right to."

I want to slap him in his stupid face.

But then he says, "The boy may leave if he wishes. I shall not stop him."

Riotous feelings of shock and delight twirl in my belly, but when I look at Artemis, the joy falls from my face and a leaden weight settles in my stomach.

Artemis kicks at something on the carpet and stuffs his hands into the pockets of his torn jeans. "I don't belong here anymore," he mutters.

"What do you mean? This is your home."

When he looks at me, I can see the sincerity in his eyes, but he doesn't reply to me, instead turning his attention to Kincaid.

"If it's all the same to you, Mr. Kincaid, I think I'd like to go back with you and Paige."

Kincaid considers Artemis for a moment and then nods, leaving the room without another word.

I'm not sure what to say, and Artemis busies himself with re-checking a small table he already looked over, so I know he doesn't want to talk about it. Perhaps I should feel guilty about it, but I'm overwhelmingly glad he's going to stay, and I just want to hug him, but I know he'd only be grossed out by the sentiment. Teenage boys...

"Don't bother with the room to the right," I call after Kincaid, hearing his footfalls down the hall. "It's mine. There won't be anything useful inside."

Though, I've told Kincaid not to bother, my room is exactly where I head next, eager to leave Ford's. It's almost unrecognizable though. Much like Ford's, it's been entirely torn apart. My books lie in a sea of cracked spines and torn pages over the carpet, and I think that may be the worst part.

Each one is a memory of a life I wished I could have been living instead of my own. Hell, even the characters in dystopias had lives that seemed preferable to my own.

Aside from the books, the only other thing I have any care in the world for is my blanket. I take my time folding the heavy fabric, grinning as I hear the beads inside shifting this way and that.

. . .

Ford bought it by accident for himself. Before, I'd been using a threadbare quilt. I think he thought an awkward, heavy blanket would be a form of punishment.

At first, I thought it was, too. But after the first week or so I got used to it. After a month had passed, I couldn't sleep without it.

"What's that?" Artemis asks, wandering into the room. "This your room?"

"*Was* my room," I correct him. "And it's weighted. It helps me sleep."

My tone is defensive, and I think Art picks up on it because he raises his brows. "I wasn't implying anything."

"Didn't say you were."

"Okay," he says, drawing out the word as he pushes his fingers to the industrial locking mechanism on my door. It's broken now, but it's clear to see that it isn't the normal sort of thing you'd find on a little girl's bedroom door. The coded keypad is on the outside. Meant to lock the person in rather than to lock intruders out. "Guess I'll go see if Kincaid needs help downstairs."

"Downstairs?" I choke out, my heart racing as I shoulder past him into the hall.

Kincaid hovers at the top of the stairs, and I hold out my hand as though I'm about to physically stop him, but I can't make my feet move more than another inch in their direction.

"Don't," I say in a breath. "You won't find anything down there. It's empty."

White-hot shame rises to my face, and Kincaid must sense my panic because he pauses. "What is it?"

"I just…I know there's nothing down there."

It's a lie, and I think he can sense it. There's a filing cabinet. A locked one in the room with the chair. Ford used to absently finger through pages of yellowing paper while the dead things and the chair did his work of terrifying and hurting me.

"I'll only be a moment," he replies before being swallowed up by the shadows down the stairs.

"Are you okay?"

"What?" I ask, trying to piece together whatever Artemis just asked me. I can't stop staring at the darkness below. I half expect it to grow arms and grab me. Swallow me whole.

"I-I need to go outside," I stammer, bunching up the heavy weighted blanket in my arms as I rush from the house, only able to properly fill my lungs once I'm outside.

"Don't touch me!" I hiss when Artemis places a hand on my back, and then. "I'm sorry, it's just…I just…"

"All good. You don't have to explain."

I've only just managed to catch my breath, counting to three in my head when a loud bang inside snatches away my composure once more.

A feral roar from below precedes Kincaid's exit

from the house. His footfalls on the stairs are like an approaching Godzilla, and I know before I see him that he's in his demon form. He storms from the house, yellow eyes blazing in a face that's devoid of all color, even under the light of the sun.

Heat radiates out from his pores, shimmering in the air around him.

"Let's go," he bellows, nearly ripping the door off the sedan parked in the driveway as he folds his large form into the driver's seat. "*Now!*"

6

Kincaid barely leaves his room for days. He exits only for liquor or to speak to his henchmen, who come to the door with news or seeking commands almost three times a day now. I can hear him in the night, too, pacing in the halls.

At first, I thought he was absently wandering the house, simply unable to sleep. But he only walks the hallway leading past my bedroom, and his footfalls slow noticeably as he passes.

Checking to see that I'm still in the house?

I'm not sure.

If he wanted to speak to me, he would. Kincaid doesn't strike me as the type to not speak his mind on any subject, so I don't know why he hesitates if that is the case.

He was clearly disgusted by what he saw down

there. The angels will have already taken what they wanted from the filing cabinet so there would only have been the remnant of animal corpses scattered around an electric chair. A pressurized hose in the cement room with the rusted drain in the floor. Bits of my skin caught in the uneven surfaces. Ford's torture instruments. His coffee machine.

He thinks me weak. Pathetic.

I could see it in the set of his eyes when he came out of Ford's house. They blazed with a loathing so potent that I couldn't get the image out of my head. Not even in sleep.

A part of me wants to explain to him that I tried. *I tried* to escape. Many times. And each of those times I was punished. The few times I got far enough to beg someone for help, Ford had the documentation to prove my insanity.

People would smile and nod, looking on with pity as he dragged me back to his truck, kicking and screaming. They would do nothing as I beat my fists bloody against the bulletproof glass windows, tears streaming down my face.

It was an ugly truth, what he did to me. People would rather believe a beautifully constructed lie.

But would he understand?

I'm not that girl anymore. Well, part of her still clings to my bones and hides in the corners of my mind, but she's fading. I'm being something...other. Different.

Stronger, I hope.

"Are you even going to try?" Artemis asks, and I tuck my crossed legs in tighter, giving my head a little shake.

Art and I have constructed a schedule of sorts since our silent return to the mansion. In the morning, I make breakfast and we eat together in the dining room. In the afternoon, I read from the book on Necromancy—well, the pages in the common tongue that I can understand. And then after lunch we work on whatever it is I learned from reading earlier in the day.

I made the mistake of slacking on my learning once and almost paid the price by not being prepared when a spirit tried to get a foothold in my head. I'm not about to let that happen again, not when there's something I can do to prepare myself against it.

Besides, it provides a welcome distraction from the demon smashing things up in his bedroom down the hall.

I wonder if he'll let me go now? If he's realized just how useless I'll be to him, even once I've learned to wield this demonic power in my blood.

"Yeah, hang on. Just give me a minute."

Practicing on Artemis is easy because his soul is so bright and vivid with life, but I doubt accomplishing the same feats on a Diablim soul will have the same effect.

I can now feel the edges of his soul. The difference between it and his body—where bone and sinew end and soul begins. This is step one to removing a soul from the keeper's body, but I'm not yet brave enough to experiment with step two. If I fuck something up, Artemis' soul could fully detach, and I risk not being able to re-deposit it in time to save him from bodily decay.

"I've got it," I whisper, trying not to break focus. It's warm and soft, like Casper's fur whispering against my cheeks.

Speak of the devil...

A plaintive *meow* sounds on the other side of my door followed by the scratching of claws. My focus is broken, and I release Art's hands, falling back on my own for a rest.

"Should I let him in?"

"I vote no, but we both know you don't listen to anything I say, so..."

I roll my eyes at him.

He's been beseeching me to go talk to Kincaid, but I don't know what I'd say, and I'm not sure I want to face him just yet. Better to let him get his raging revulsion out of his system first. Then, I'm sure, he'll come to me.

Huffing, I rise and open the door, letting Casper scamper inside. He stretches up on his hind legs, pulling at the woven denim in my jeans with his claws until a few strands come loose and I give in, lifting him from the floor.

"I don't know why Kincaid is so angry that I named

you," I coo, nuzzling the top of his horned head with my chin. "It's just a name."

"I'm sure there's a reason," Artemis says in a low voice to himself, knowing full well that I can hear him. I tried to distance myself from the demon housecat when we first arrived back, but it proved ever more difficult since he didn't seem to want to leave me alone. And truly, I didn't feel right keeping him separate.

He was quickly becoming more *my* cat than Kincaid. I felt a strange sort of responsibility for him. Or maybe *ownership* was the correct word.

"If you're done practicing, I need a snack."

"We literally just ate."

He shrugs. "So?"

I set Casper down on the bed, and he hisses at Artemis, white tail twitching this way and that upon my weighted blanket like a pendulum of doom.

"I think that thing is going to feast on my bones someday," Artemis muses with a look of disgust on his angelic face. He's really filled out over the past couple weeks. His cheeks are less sallow and his shoulders seem more broad. More aligned with the size a boy his age should be. Or what I think it should be. I don't have much to compare it to.

"Stop it, he's fine. Who's my good boy, Casper, hmmm?"

He rolls to his belly, and I give him a quick rub. "There's just one more thing I want to try, but if I'm understanding the text correctly, then it might wear you out."

His brows pinch. "Like, how?"

"Like I need to pull from your spirit energy to be able to do it."

"Pull from Casper's."

"He's barely got any," I reply, letting my eyes go unfocused so I can just make out the faintest green aura around Casper on the bed. "If I pull what he has it might kill the poor thing."

"What a shame that would be."

"Art!"

"Fine, okay. Just do the thing, but can you *please* ask Kincaid to get one of his henchmen to volunteer for spirit lessons every once in a while?"

"Why, do you have something better to do?"

"Actually, yes. I do."

I don't ask what that is. I don't think I want to know what he does in his messy bedroom with all the shutters closed and the door locked.

"Fine."

I take his hand and slump back down to the carpet. I have no intention of asking Kincaid for a guinea pig to practice on. Not because I wouldn't rather drain the spirit energy from someone other than Art—because I would prefer that. No, because I don't trust anyone else.

Not how I trust Artemis.

I need my full focus to be on the task to accomplish

anything with this ability. I can't focus if I don't trust the person sitting opposite me.

"Just relax," I tell him, inhaling through my nose and exhaling through my mouth, trying to find that center of being deep within that the text talks about. "I'll draw only as much as I need."

This is what I read about earlier today. A way to shut out the voices in my head by ever so slightly detaching my own soul. I didn't understand it well, and I blame the fact that half the page was in the runic demon language, but I think I got the gist.

Just like I could feel Artemis' soul beneath his skin, I could also feel my own when I tried. But when I used my power to work on his soul, I drew from my own spirit energy. Now, trying to accomplish something with my own soul, I needed to borrow the energy from Artemis.

Or at least, I assume that's what the complicated inked diagram on the page means.

I envision Artemis' spirit like it's made of water and picture it flowing out from his palm and into mine. A slow, steady stream. I don't want to drain him too much.

It takes far longer than I care to admit, but after a time there's a tingle in my palm and my fingers twitch against his wrist as a radiant warmth clambers from palm to wrist, wrist to elbow, and then settles somewhere in my center like a blanket for my soul.

It's comforting. Invigorating.

I try to remember exactly what the text said and almost lose the budding spirit energy, having to claw it back.

Crap.

Throwing caution to the wind, I attempt to *will* my spirit to detach.

Shut the voices up.

Shut the voices up.

Shut them out.

I repeat the words like a mantra or a spell, trying to guide my spirit to detach the correct way in order to accomplish the end I desire. If I pull it back too far, I'm truly not sure what will happen.

Like a valve bursting from too much pressure, the dam holding the voices back in my skull crumples. Distantly, I hear Artemis cry out, but I'm rushing to shove them back. Trying to find the seam of my soul to pull it back over the endless expanse of crowding dead.

No!

A cacophonous laugh crackles in my head, followed by a *snap* and *hiss*. The loudest of the voices grow in volume and intensity, and I buckle under their assault. They're warring with one another, vying for command.

"Paige!"

A crashing sound beyond the blackness of my vision is followed by the rain of plaster on hardwood.

"What's happening?" Kincaid thunders. "Let go of her."

"*No*," I howl. I need Artemis' energy to seal it back up. To undo whatever the hell I've just horribly messed up, but I can't say that. If I speak again, I'll lose the tenuous grip I still have and there'll be a spiritual free-for-all in my fucking head.

Kincaid grips my chin and I lose it.

The control slips through my fingers, and I feel it. I feel *him* battle to the surface. He slides into me like a knife slides through flesh. With a little resistance at first, and then nothing to stop him.

I fall back. There, but not there.

My body slumps. Heavy. All bones and blood with no idea how the parts work together anymore.

And then nothing.

I feel nothing.

I *am* nothing.

Just a bystander as my hand comes free from Artemis' and he falls unconscious to the floor. Forced to watch as my body, no longer my own, gets unsteadily to its feet. The world tipping and turning through the shared vision of my eyes.

Reflected in Kincaid's horror-stricken gaze, I do not see myself. I see the rugged, beard coated jawline of a man. His short hair and hooked nose.

His stubby fingers and deep blue eyes.

~~He~~ *I* stagger forward, arms outstretched for Kincaid's throat, a strangled cry lodged in my throat. I'm powerless to stop it, screaming inside as Kincaid dodges the attack, sweeping my legs out from under my body. I don't feel pain as my hip connects with the wooden floor.

I can see Kincaid. I can hear him grunting. I can smell his hickory and musk scent as he climbs on top of my body and pins my arms and legs to the floor. I can taste blood in my mouth.

But I *feel* nothing.

"Paige!" Kincaid demands, his eyes wild as he struggles against the inhuman strength of ~~my~~ *his* defense.

"Come back to me!"

"Fuck you!" The words are from my own lips, but I didn't speak them.

"Send him back!" Kincaid demands again, getting a stronger hold on my lurching, bucking hips with his groin pressed firmly down against my waist. "Do it now!"

I can't, I cry inside; panic makes doing anything other than watching impossible.

Calm down—I need to calm down.

One…

Let the fear in.

Two…

Deep breath. Am I even the one breathing?

Three…

Push him the fuck out.

"Get out of her, or I will drag your soul to Hell and see to your torture personally, you worthless scum,"

Kincaid grinds out, his horns protruding from his skull as his demon form finishes taking over.

The transformation gives me the opportunity I need. My body has stopped fighting. The spirit in my mind, a man so vile I can feel the stain of his soul leaving marks on my own, has lost his foothold. Kincaid's demon form has startled him enough that I can feel my mistake.

A gap in an otherwise solid tapestry.

The slit in my soul it got through.

It takes all of my energy to will it shut. To will the bastard out and refill the gap. When it's done, I'm left staring up into twin suns.

The weight of myself is so much that I'm afraid I might break right through the floor and keep falling. Pain sizzles in my wrists and across my hip bones. My head feels like it's been hollowed out with a spoon, and I just want everything to stop.

A moment later, it does. I hear the reassuring whisper of a demon at my ear and the press of a warm forehead against mine as I drift away.

THEIR RAISED VOICES WAKE ME, AND I WANT TO COVER my ears but moving my hands feels like moving cinder blocks, so instead I hiss, "Stop shouting," though admittedly it sounds more like an unintelligible mumble, my tongue lazy and lips refusing to open.

"She's awake!"

"You…okay?" I ask, trying to find the seam of my eyelids in the broken neuro pathways of my mind to open them. I remember how he fell. How his eyes rolled back in his head when I finally let go, having used up all the spirit energy he could give.

"Me? Are you fucking serious?"

"Don't…curse."

"Is she for real?"

"*Na'vazēm?*" Kincaid croons, and I find the will to open my eyes, searching in the clouded space to my right for his face.

"That *sucked.*"

He barks a laugh, but I can see how it doesn't reach his eyes as mine begin to clear and the feeling returns to the lower half of my body.

Artemis gives me a knowing look. "No shit, Sherlock."

"I'm sorry. I didn't mean to drain you."

"Are you in danger now?" Kincaid asks, his eyes fixated on my own, as though through sheer force of will he can make me give him the answer he craves.

I give my head a little shake. "No, I don't think so. The spirits are back to being annoying flies on the wall."

I try to sit up and fall back down. Artemis mutters that I should rest because he doesn't have the energy to heal me yet, but Kincaid slides a hand under my back, pressing up between my shoulder blades to help me to sitting.

My head spins, but otherwise, I can already feel the weighted, icky feeling sloughing away.

Kincaid's fingers curve on my back, and I resist the urge to press harder into them. The way they whisper against my skin is doing all kinds of things to my belly that I just can't handle right now.

"We're going to need to do something about your abilities."

"What?" Artemis asks, surprising me with how at ease he seems at the moment. Separated from Kincaid by only me and a small channel of mattress where I lie propped by Kincaid on my bed.

I wonder if my offer to set him free has anything to do with it. Kincaid was prepared to let him go and Artemis made the conscious decision to remain. And Kincaid let him. He's no longer just a purchased piece of property, but something more.

I wouldn't go so far as to call him a guest, but we're getting there.

"Her power is growing too rapidly, and she needs to know how to control it," Kincaid continues. "I think I have an idea, but it may not work."

I didn't like the sound of that. He didn't seem to like whatever he was thinking of to solve this little problem either.

"How soon will you be able to heal her?" he asks Art. "We'll need to make a little trip to The Freakshow tonight."

Artemis startles as though struck. "Um," he

mumbles. "If I get some food and water, maybe like an hour?"

"Good."

The Freakshow? I knew that name. Where had I heard it before?

"Do you want to come with us?" I ask Artemis, and by the way he stills, I already know his answer.

He shakes his head and stands, rushing to get off the bed on shaky limbs. "Hard pass."

He leaves, and I hear the thuds as he stomps down the stairs outside.

"It's where my men found him," Kincaid tells me in a low voice. "They were using him to heal the wounded in one of the fighting pits. He was unconscious in the mud when they purchased him from the Old Crones."

A furious heat unspools in my belly, and I clench my teeth. I wonder if they are still there, but I don't ask. I'm afraid of what I'll do with the information. A chant of murderous intent plays on a reel in the background of my thoughts, and I just know that if I let myself go there, I won't be able to come back.

"You're certain the spirits are held at bay?" Kincaid asks for a second time, and I offer him a small half-grin.

"I'm sure." I pause, fiddling with the edge of my blanket, gathering up the courage to ask what I've been afraid to for days now. "What happened at Ford's house…what you saw down there, I just want you to know that I am *not* weak. I tried to escape."

The words come out in a flood now, and I can't seem to dam them.

"I tried so many times and every time I failed, and I—"

"Don't," he cautions and shame heats my face.

Kincaid's hand falls from my back, and I shiver, suddenly cold.

"I couldn't understand it," he says, and it's clear it pains him to tell me this. I almost want to cover my ears to keep from hearing it, knowing he has the power to undo me more than Ford ever did. I learned to barricade my heart away from the things Ford said. The things he did.

My heart isn't barricaded anymore, not against Kincaid. The carefully crafted ironwork built up over the twenty-two years of my life has been destroyed. I try to rebuild it day by day, but the work is half-hearted, and it shows.

"Couldn't understand what?"

"Your shame," he says, and my brows draw together. "I've done terrible things, Paige. Things you couldn't even imagine."

He's stoic as he tells me this. No trace of shame or regret for his crimes. Just a reluctant acceptance of them.

"But being forced to see what was done to you—and then to know that you somehow blame yourself for it...I didn't understand. I still don't. How could you feel shame for something that was inflicted on you?

For something you were unwillingly forced to endure?"

"I..." I don't know what to say.

Kincaid brushes a thumb over my jaw, and I press my cheek into his warm palm, feeling stripped bare to the bone under the microscope of his stare.

"You didn't deserve the life you lived before you came here."

"And the people you did bad things to—they *did* deserve it?"

His hand falls. "Yes."

He lifts a glass of water from the bedside table and presses it into my hand. At the same time, Casper jumps up onto the bed with a stuttering yowl and comes to nudge his horned head against my arm. He must've left with all the commotion and only just come back.

"So, are you going to tell me why you're so angry about me naming the cat?"

Kincaid glares at the cat, his jaw flexing.

It stares right back with an almost knowing expression on its feline face. It's unsettling, even more so as his tail stills.

"It isn't a cat, *Na'vazēm.*"

"I know, it's demonic."

Kincaid gives his head a small shake. "It's chosen that form. It has another."

My skin bristles where Casper still touches me, and

when I look at him, I find he's also looking up at me, tail twitching against the blanket again.

"It's a demon, Paige. A powerful one. Which is the only reason I've allowed it to remain here in the house. As a sort of insurance, should I ever need it."

"I'm not following."

Kincaid licks his lips, and if he didn't just tell me the harmless looking kitty pawing my arm was a powerful *demon,* my panties would be melting.

"It's chosen this house as it's home in the mortal world. It will defend it against attack. It's why I knew you would be safe here even when I was not."

His gaze darkens.

"The whole of Elisium knows it's here."

A cold nose presses to my knuckles, and I shudder, lifting my hands out of Casper's reach.

"What *kind* of demon is it, exactly?"

"An ancient one. Older than me. Older than Lucifer. It resided in the bowels of Hell long before God cast his golden son from the heavens and forced him into a seat of power in the underworld."

I can't breathe.

"And in naming it." He pauses, and I want to shake him to make him finish speaking. Danger pulses in my chest. A staccato rhythm that makes stars explode at the edges of my vision and my hands tremble. "You've bound it to you."

"Bound it to me? What do you mean?"

Kincaid's fists clench on his lap, black to the knuckles.

"In exchange for your soul, it will do your bidding. If near, it will protect you from harm. And you may draw power from it. A great deal of power. But each time you do, it will consume a small piece of your soul...until there is nothing left."

7

"It's simple then," I rush to say as Kincaid and I pile into the driver's and passenger seat of his car later that night. "I just won't draw any power from it."

Kincaid gives me a sad smile but nods. "That would be wise."

"Why are you looking at me like that?"

He pulls out of the driveway and onto the main road, dodging a newly fallen branch.

"You shouldn't have been able to bind it. The soul of a Diablim isn't strong enough. And even if it were, it wouldn't be enough to tempt the demon into accepting the bargain."

"But I didn't even *know* I was binding it to me when I named it. Isn't that, like, force majeure, or something? Can't I get out of this bargain?"

"I'm afraid not."

I groan inwardly and settle back into my seat, rolling the window down for some air. "Wait…I'm a Necromancer. So my type of magic deals with souls. What if I can take whatever part of my soul it has back and break the bond?"

"That's what I've been trying to find more information on," Kincaid admits. "It's why my men have been stopping by the house, and it's why I'm taking you to The Freakshow. I don't think you will be able to break the bond, but you may be able to make it work to your advantage instead of the demon's."

I cross my arms over my chest. "Or we could just kill it."

I hate how that makes my stomach sour. No matter what creature lurks beneath the surface of Casper's fur-coated skin, he's still an adorable cat. One that has kept me company at night while I slept and lent me comfort while Kincaid was gone and I didn't know if he would return.

It's a betrayal, knowing now that it likely never wanted to comfort me at all, it wanted me to claim it.

So that it could claim me.

The car comes to a jarring stop, and I have to throw my hands forward to keep from flinging into the dashboard. "What are you—"

"*You cannot kill it.*" He seethes. "If the demon dies, so will you."

I search for any trace of jest in his tone but there is none. His hands wring the steering wheel.

I bite my lip. "And what if I die? What happens to it?"

He doesn't reply to that straight away, just puts the car back into gear and continues down the dark road. "I'm going to ensure that doesn't happen."

"If you just told me about the demon then this wouldn't have happened."

It's cruel and it's too-little-too-late to point out, but I can't stop myself from saying the words. It's the truth.

"You think I don't know that?" he asks in a dead monotone. "If the last of the time-turning demons wasn't lost to the Otherworld, I'd have already summoned one to fix this."

I have no idea what he's rambling about, but I don't care. I just hope he knows now that keeping things from me is *not* a good idea.

He doesn't need a name, that's what Kincaid told me. Not, *by the way,* Na'vazēm, *if you name the demon, your soul will be bound to it for eternity, and it will eat tiny pieces of it until you die.*

If I'd fucking known that, I wouldn't have made friends with it. *Ugh.*

"We're nearly there, I need you to—"

"Yeah, yeah." I wave him off. "Don't leave your side, I know the drill."

I swear I can hear his teeth grinding.

"What are we even doing there?"

"Speaking to the only Necromancer I know in Elisium. His Diablim bloodline is weak, making him entirely useless in this situation—"

"Then why are we speaking to him?" I interrupt, throwing my hands in the air before crossing them back against my chest, tighter than they were before—to hold in my ever-growing rage.

"If you'd let me finish, then you would know," he snarls at me. "Do *not* roll your eyes at me."

"Or what?"

He takes a long, shuddering breath before the black taint on his hands recedes, though his horns—they remain. I never noticed how iridescent they are. The black shot through with bits of indigo and silver in the faint moonlight.

"We are going to speak to him because he is the only Diablim in Elisium who knows the whereabouts of Lady Devereaux."

I wonder if he can feel the daggers I'm trying to shoot at him with my eyes. As if I should just *know* who that is or why we need to find her.

"Are you going to tell me who that is or should I take a wild guess?"

He raises a brow at my sarcasm, and something flips in my belly. He's…*amused*. It suits him.

Kincaid reaches over me and rolls up my window as lights flash and blaze in the distance. The curve of a

Ferris wheel lifts above the tops of trees to our right, and through the branches I can see the brightly colored fabric of tents and the movement of bodies.

He might have shut the window, but I can smell it from here. A salty sweetness with an undercurrent of something rotten. I can hear it, too. Shouts of glee. Of anguish. A riot of chatter all mushing together into one vibrant hum rising and falling with the drumming beat of music.

"Lady Devereaux is a Necromancer. The most powerful one who's ever lived. And she owes me a debt."

"Why doesn't anyone else know where she is?"

"She's retired."

My face screws up into a scowl trying to picture a retired Diablim. What would that even look like? Was she just out there somewhere reading books and knitting scarves, chatting with the spirits in her head for company?

The reality of what sort of life lies before me hits me like a wet slap across the face.

"*Na'vazēm,* what is it?"

"Hmm?"

The multicolored lights wrapping an archway paint his face in shades of red and blue, glinting off his horns as we pass beneath.

A crush of Diablim disperse as Kincaid parks in the middle of the throughway and steps out of the driver's side. He's around the car and opening my door before I can even reach for the handle. I want to ask him if he really intends to just leave his car right there in the middle of the entrance, but then I remember who it is I'm speaking to.

The Diablim gasp and whisper, giving Kincaid and me a wide berth as he loops his arm through mine and tugs me along. A female Diablim pulls the arm of her child when he tries to peer into the driver's side window of the car, giving him hell for getting so close.

"I'm not sure I should have brought you here," Kincaid whispers in a voice so low I'm fairly sure no one around us would hear him. I don't reply, but I'm inclined to agree.

By the way the Diablim here are watching not just their lord, but *me,* I can tell they know exactly who I am. Word has traveled fast. I could understand why Kincaid would be regretting his very *final* decision about not letting me out of his sight.

The souls of the Diablim around me vary in brightness, I notice. Some shining dully, flickering like small flames on short wicks. Others pulse with a steadier glow. And others still hold almost no glow at all.

I know now what it means. The ones with the brighter souls are less Diablim and more mortal. And the ones with almost no light within have much stronger demonic bloodlines. They are the ones to steer clear of. The most dangerous of them.

Here and there, interspersed throughout, there are

Nephilim, too. A gargoyle, I think as I take in the ashen skin of a middle-aged man with violet eyes. Another with a sweep of auburn hair and an aura like starlight watches me with a keen interest that makes my stomach clench and the blood leech from my fingertips.

"Fresh meat!" A thick voice calls, and I turn, nearly run over by a Diablim man carrying a tray of sizzling tubes of meat, but Kincaid jerks me roughly out of the way and flips the tray of meat into the face of its carrier. He screeches as the meat scalds his rotund face and neck, but falls to his knees and goes silent immediately upon seeing who he's accosted.

"Forgive me, my lord," he cries in a high pitch. "Please. I have children."

I'm honestly not sure I trust that Kincaid won't kill the Diablim man on his knees simply for *almost* bumping into me. I thread my fingers through his and give a little pull. "Let's go find that Necro."

He lingers for a second, undiluted rage simmering beneath the surface of his stare before he allows me to guide him forward again, and the Diablim man on the ground dissolves into whimpering sobs at our backs.

I try to ignore the stares and whispers as we pass, part of me wishing I'd worn something a little more—well, a little *more* than the low cut, cropped top and torn jeans that barely fit my waist. They hang down so low they show the bevel and dip of my hip bones.

Beside Kincaid in his debonair jacket, crisp linen

shirt, and regal bearing, I probably look like a street urchin. Or something much worse.

Instead of focusing on them, I try to look instead at the wares in the tents. They're easily distracting. Little packages of what looks like miniature wings. Lightly glowing bottles, the liquid contained within bubbling without having been touched. Crystals of all shapes, colors, and sizes. Runic carvings and roasted street rats.

The noises ahead begin to overtake the hushed chatter and music floating over the market. Screams of delight and pain, snarls and a bark, the sounds I'd heard from the car. As we break through the last of the tents, my eyes widen to an open space.

Carnival rides tip and spin, carrying passengers whose eyes gleam with exhilaration and the shine of intoxication. A large Diablim man with a burned face thumbs through a wad of bills, passing out the winnings of a bet.

Dug into the ground are pits all around, ringed in iron railings. Jeering, shouting Diablim crush against the iron bars, concealing what lies within. I wander toward one, catching a glimpse of orange glow and the flick of a black tail before Kincaid jerks me back.

"Do not wander," he warns, scanning the Diablim mob in search of the Necromancer boy.

"What are they doing?" I ask, unable to help myself.

He blinks at me as though he's only just realizing

what I've said, too distracted with keeping an eye on everything and everyone around us.

"The fighting pits," he tells me. "Hellhounds there." He points at the one where I saw the flick of a tail. "Diablim there." He points to another where a blood-curdling scream rises from within, and the ground around the ring cheers.

"Come, the boy will be this way."

I let him take me away from the awful sounds and the faint smell of beer and piss, through the carnival rides seeming to operate without the need for electricity, and to a smaller channel of performers.

A Nephilim girl clasps the hand of an older man sitting opposite a table, she recants to him a story that I think is one of his own memories. How odd. Perhaps he has a faulty memory? She's a diviner then. I remember the one who the officer back in St. Louis proper sent in to glean information from me and shudder.

That diviner was the reason I wound up here in the first place.

Another diviner occupies the tent next to that one and I go still, taking in the people—two girls and a boy sitting around the table. Their auras aren't the starlit brightness of Nephilim, nor are they the flickering glow of a Diablim's.

"Are they human?"

Kincaid considers the people at the table, giggling at

whatever the handsome diviner boy is telling them. "Yes. They come across the barrier to the west. It's only a few miles from here. Mortals keep fresh cashflow coming into Elisium. They come at their own peril, but the Diablim know their value. They'll likely not be harmed so long as they're spending."

"What idiots."

"Were you not curious about the devil's playground across the water, *Na'vazēm?*"

I want to tell him I would never have been stupid enough to tempt fate by coming here, but I'm not sure that's true. I sat outside Ford's bedroom door with a hand clamped over my mouth to silence my breaths just to hear Lacey Lewis from the evening news tell me more about Elisium and the creatures that lived here.

I'd always been fascinated by it. By *them*.

"That's what I thought," he says with a smug smirk, his hand squeezing mine. "Here we are. It's just up ahead."

A small crowd of maybe nine or ten people create a jagged barrier to the tent Kincaid pulls me toward, and I stand on tiptoe to see over their heads. The smell reaches me first, and I gag, trying to pull back from the tent. But Kincaid has already cleared his throat, and the grouping of six humans and a couple of Diablim part, casting curious stares at my demon lord.

With the curtain of their bodies drawn back, there's nothing to block the view within. He's certainly a showman, this Necromancer. With his green-hued lighting and the smoke machine carefully tucked away in one corner of the tent, spewing wispy curls of gray smog over the procession of dead things.

His reflective eyes dance as he grins down at his abominations. A squirrel with dull black eyes and part of its torso missing, revealing a delicate set of ribs pressed so close together they look like the teeth of a comb.

A cat, standing on its hind legs, with oozing wounds across its belly and throat. It's missing both its eyes, but that doesn't stop it from walking about, doing a strange little jig at the behest of its puppet master.

The mortals cringe and squeal, both disgusted and delighted at once as they drop bills and coins into an upturned top hat on a chair.

"More!" one calls. "Do something bigger!"

"Yeah, like a bear!" another adds, clasping her pale hands together with a wild grin. Her aura has an odd, muted quality and with one look at her eyes, the pupils almost entirely taking over the irises, I know she's heavily intoxicated. I hope she's on human drugs. I can't even imagine the sorts they would have here for their own kind.

"You want bigger?" The Necromancer calls, lifting his arms and showing off the holes in the armpits of his tattered suit jacket. He's young. Or at least, I think he is. Though his eyes are youthful, his face has a weathered quality to it that could be the product of age or circumstance, it's anyone's guess.

"The show is over," Kincaid says, leveling a hard stare on the guy who is only now noticing the presence of his lord. The color drains from his face and his arms fall. The dead things on the ground at his feet fall too, twitching and sniffling until they go still.

8

I close my eyes against the assault of a thousand memories. A thousand times I've seen the same thing and had no idea it was my own doing. I thought Ford was torturing me, trying to frighten me. When in fact he was testing the scope of my power and trying to condition me against it.

I don't find this amusing. Not in the slightest.

My hands ball, and I shoulder one of the loud-mouthed humans out of my way to take my place next to Kincaid. "Get out of here," I growl at them, hardly recognizing my own voice. "Leave this place and don't come back."

The intoxicated girl lifts her hands, and fear rounds her eyes as she stumbles back from me. "Wh-what is she?" she cries, and I wonder what it is she sees that frightens her. I don't get to ask though as she takes off like a shot and her fear spurs the others to leave. Must be the drugs.

I watch as the few Diablim who'd been around them compare their spoils and realize that they'd only been there to pick the idiots' pockets, not to enjoy the show.

Kincaid steps over the dead things and into the tent, drawing the front flap shut behind us.

"To what do I owe this pleasure, Master Kincaid?" the guy asks, his throat bobbing as he picks at the lint on his jacket. "I don't believe I've ever had the pleasure befo—"

"Where is Lady Devereaux?"

"I don't know."

Kincaid's tail flicks out, brushing against my calf as his demon form takes over. In the green lighting, with smoke coiling around his ankles, I have to admit, it's almost comical. Strange, but it doesn't frighten me, not when the rage of his beast form is directed squarely at someone else.

"She'll kill me," the Necromancer amends. "Please. I can't—"

"You *will*."

Seemingly for the first time, the necromancer notices me beside Kincaid, and his lips part. He stares without trying to conceal his curiosity.

A sliver of unease pinching in my gut, I wonder what he sees.

The Necromancer gestures vaguely at me. "You aren't what I imagined."

Lady Devereaux seemingly forgotten for the moment, Kincaid steps protectively forward, putting himself slightly in front of me. "What *did* you imagine?" Kincaid demands.

"Word is that she's a Necro, but obviously that's bullshit."

"What do you mean?" I ask, and the Necro guy can tell, perhaps from the question or the tick in Kincaid's jaw, that he's made some sort of mistake because he backtracks, shaking his head.

"I just mean that her soul isn't, *um,* as dark as it should be, I guess."

Kincaid already had a similar suspicion, given that the demon hiding in the body of Casper jumped at the chance to bond itself to me.

He and I share a look before he turns back to the Necro with a renewed fury ignited by his frustration. He grips the guy by the front of his shirt, lifting him two feet from the ground with ease. "I won't ask again, boy. Where can I find Lady Deveraux? According to my contacts you are the only worthless corpse in Elisium who knows."

The guy recoils as if anticipating a strike and seals his eyes shut. "She's in Infernum," he squeals. "Living beyond the edge of the city, but within the boundary. That's all I know."

Kincaid growls like an animal, and the guy

screeches as if he were a child. "A blue house," he adds. "With a rose garden. East side."

"If you're lying—"

"I-I'm not, I swear. She used to drag me over there, you know, in my spirit form. For updates about Elisium."

"When was the last time she summoned you?"

"I don't know, maybe a year? More?"

Kincaid frowns, but drops the guy back to the soiled ground. He doesn't try to rise, he just half lies, half sits there, among his putrid smelling dead things.

"You will not warn her of my coming," he tells the Necromancer.

"Of course, my lord. I won't say a word."

"What do you think he meant?" I ask Kincaid once we're clear of the quieter entertainment and are looping back through the louder carnival rides. "About my soul not being like a Necromancer's?"

"I cannot tell you. I have several theories, but none make much sense. I'm confident Lady Devereaux will have the answers."

"How are we going to get to Infernum?"

"We?"

I'm about to tell him I'd rather not be left alone at the house with a demonic cat *thing* for protection, but someone catches my eye.

A girl lying in the dirt at the edge of a fighting pit. She can't be more than eleven. Her aura is bright but waning. I'm not sure how I know, but I do. She's dying.

Without making the conscious decision to, I find I'm already halfway to her. Kincaid tries to stop me, but I twist out of his grasp. She's Nephilim, I'm sure of it.

I push through the throng, trying to get to her as Diablim block my view.

"Make them move," I beseech Kincaid without bothering to check he's heard me. "She needs help."

An old Diablim woman with a hooked nose and a sneer reaches her first, gripping her roughly by her shoulder to flip her over. The Nephilim girl's aura wanes and flickers, grows smaller by the second.

The old woman shakes her, and I can hear her nasally voice shouting. She slaps the girl across her face, and the smallest whimper croaks from her lips.

Her eyes roll back as I reach her, and the light in her soul splutters, going out like a snuffed wick. The old woman drops the girl with disgust and sneers to another, equally hideous and beady eyed twin to her right. "Dead," she says. "Useless. I *told* you we should have bought the elder of the two."

It's then that I recognize them and something inside of me snaps.

They are the women who bought Artemis.

This Nephilim girl is just the latest in what is most likely a string of dead innocents forced into slavery in Elisium.

"Crones!" Comes a throaty bellow, and I see a giant horned demon with scalding red eyes watching the women from afar. His voice booms, cutting through all the others. "Heal your opponent or withdraw."

The Old Crone kicks the corpse of the girl and unleashes a feral cry, tossing her hands up. "Withdraw!"

She would do more than that.

Distantly, I can hear Kincaid behind me, telling me he would deal with them, but I'm not listening. My skin tingles all over as I draw in energy like pulling water through a sieve.

I can see their souls. Dirty, vile things. Barely there, but just enough to grip on to as I feel for their edges. A foul taste like rotten fruit coats my tongue and slithers into my belly, making it roil but I do not stop.

I do not stop when each of the Crones is gripped into stillness from my hold. Nor do I waver even when their eyes bulge and their beady pupils lock on to mine in a mixture of rage and terror. No. I revel in it. I think I may be smiling as the noises of The Freakshow hush and then spur to life anew.

What these vile women did to this girl, what they did to Artemis—they would never *do* again. I wasn't willing to gamble with pulling Artemis' soul from his body for fear that I may not be able to drop it back inside. That fear doesn't exist here.

And I have no intention of putting them back.

Pain like a battering ram knocking from temple to temple begins inside my skull, speckling my vision with stars. I remove my bracelets and drop them to the ground, finding a brand new rush of delicious power. The ground beneath my feet trembles.

I push and pull, tearing their souls from their bodies. It's like trying to pull apart the fabric of the universe. It should be impossible, and yet it comes loose thread by thread, made pliable by the grip of my power.

They fray apart until their filthy little lights go out and their lifeless corpses drop to the earth.

I come back to myself, dropping to my knees as I cough up a mixture of soul bile and blood from my throat, spitting it onto the ground.

The corpses tremble and twitch and the surrounding crowd cry out in surprise.

"The bracelets," Kincaid mutters in a dangerous tone and shoves them back on my wrist, making the reanimating corpses of the Nephilim girl and the two Diablim women go still once more.

He lifts me and my face presses against the warm dark of his chest as he bears me away at inhuman speeds. Out of the fighting pits. Out through the trees. Until The Freakshow is only a muted glow in the distance. Until the voices are indistinguishable from the deadened sound of thudding music and we are alone.

9

"N*a'vazēm?*" His rough voice summons me out from within—out from the place where I was still ensconced in power inside. It's like a tremble in my fingertips. The aftereffects of the power draw thrummed in my blood like a seductive song, trying to coerce me into using it to the last drop.

I found my corporeal body and forced my slitted eyes to open fully, rolling my head back to peer up at him.

"Are you hurt?"

I jerk my head side to side, clenching my fingers and wiggling my toes just to make sure it's the truth. My strength returns in spades as I come back into my body from wherever I'd been inside of my own mind, and I sigh against the suddenly heavy feeling in my chest.

Our eyes meet, and in them I see a likeness.

"What you did back there, anyone would have done the same. I wish you wouldn't have drawn so much attention, but do not feel guilt for—"

"What?"

Did he think I regretted it?

Slowly, I see the truth dawn in his eyes, and he looks at me strangely, like perhaps he's never seen me properly before.

"They deserved to die," I tell him, deadpan. "Just like Ford did."

I wriggle in his grip, sensing something out of place. Something doesn't feel right.

It takes me a moment to put my finger on it as Kincaid lowers us on the carpet of leaves until I'm seated on his raised knee with my feet back on the ground. It isn't me who's out of place. It's him.

"Kincaid," I say in a breath, incredulous as I press my hands to his chest, slipping them beneath the collar of his tunic to rest against his bare flesh.

He grunts but doesn't stop me as I shut my eyes, feeling with that *other* sense. The one still buzzing with unspent power in my bones. "I can feel it…"

"Feel what, *Na'vazēm?*"

"Your soul."

It flutters deep within him, and against my eyelids I can see the faintest flick of color. An iridescent blue. When I open my eyes again and meet his, I see that it clings to him on the outside, too. So faint that I'd never see it unless I was searching for it. A flicker of life. His spirit aura.

His brows draw together. "I don't have a soul, *Na'vazēm,*" he says. "Not anymore."

I smirk, bringing my hands up to his face to pull his attention back to me. "I can see it," I promise him. "It's faint. Barely a whisper. But it's there."

Something in him breaks at my words, and the mask of indifference he wears for all the rest is stripped away. He's flayed bare to me. His eyes search mine and when they fall briefly to my lips, I can't stop myself.

My hands curl around his head and slip into his black hair, brushing against the ribbed surface of his horns as I press my mouth to his. He shudders beneath me, his still part-demon hands clawing into my back in the most exquisite way. On the verge of inflicting pain, but just restrained enough to avoid it.

His chest rumbles against mine and my nipples pebble, hips arching as his hands slip beneath the hem of my shirt, rough fingertips grazing up the sensitive sides of my ribcage. A moan expands in my throat and he goes berserk.

The almost sweet kiss turns into something else entirely. His tongue slips into my mouth just as his grip on my waist tightens, lifting and lowering until my back is in the dirt and I've forgotten how to breathe. My hips lift to meet him as he settles over me, pressing firmly into the solid steel of his cock.

Another moan escapes, and he catches my lower lip between his teeth, biting and sucking as he grinds down against my sex.

The aching flutter in my belly spreads like wildfire, making my thighs clench and my cheeks flare. It's the most beautiful agony I've ever felt, and I want more.

I want it all.

I find the swell of his cock with my hand, and he groans into my mouth before moving to trace a line of fevered kisses down my throat. Palming him through his dark denim jeans isn't enough though. Not by a long shot.

I begin to undo the button, but he catches my wrists and jerks them up roughly, pinning them above my head with just one of his hands. "*No,*" he laments, his gaze wicked with a smoldering fire accented by the sharp angle of his smirk. "I want to taste you."

He silences me with one last rough kiss before he releases my hands and rocks back, dragging one clawed finger through the front of my tank top, laying me bare. My chest heaves as the cold dances over the peaks of my breast, and I gasp as his mouth closes over one, tongue swirling around the oversensitive nipple in a way that makes me cry out and bury my fists into his hair.

My cry only spurs him on, and I help him by lifting my hips as he sucks my other nipple into his mouth while his hands work to inch off my jeans. They're so big on me that it takes no effort, and he has them, and my panties, off in a flash.

A part of my mind rebels against the fact that my ass is seated firmly against damp dirt, but whatever rationality that remains is entirely silenced as he moves down, his warm breath fanning over my sex.

I buck to sitting at the intensity of the sensation, but he plants a hand firmly on my belly until I am flush against the earth once more.

He doesn't remove it, holding me still while his head lowers, leaving me to fist my hands into the dirt at my sides. Needing something to hold myself together—to keep myself tethered. Afraid to fall apart.

"Kincaid," I whimper, his name turning into a gasp on my lips as his mouth closes over me, erasing every sane thought from my mind.

He laps at my opening, using his expert tongue to bend me to his will, eliciting a long peal of ecstasy from my lungs. When his fingers push into me, adding pressure to the mind-numbing flicking of his tongue, I see stars.

He fucks me with his fingers, harder and more rapidly with each passing minute, matching the tempo of his tongue as I try and fail to stifle my cries. My body writhes beneath the hard press of his hand on my belly, hips moving in time with the thrusts of his fingers, riding the wave of ecstasy threatening to spill over my head. Swallow me whole.

"That's it, *Na'vazēm,*" he rasps, and the single second

his mouth is gone is way too long. I clutch his hair with my greedy fingers and draw him back down, wrapping my legs tightly around his shoulders. He growls as he takes me into his mouth again, this time with wild abandon until I feel a quickening begin in my core and my breath hitches.

Kincaid senses the nearness of it because he redoubles his efforts, prodding me to the edge of oblivion. I hasten over it a moment later, splintering into everything and nothing as my climax takes me. The feeling unlike anything I ever imagined. All clenching and raw and almost unbearable in its intensity.

Dark spots crowd in at the edges of my eyes as I slacken, my limbs tingling and numb as I draw into myself, breathless and gasping. Kincaid leans over me, looping his fingers around the back of my neck to hold my head up.

He kisses me, and I taste myself on his lips before he presses his forehead against mine and shuts his lust-filled eyes. "*Mea Na'vazēm.*"

"Yes," I agree. "*Yours.*"

10

The distinct silhouette of a man stands on the darkened stoop when Kincaid pulls up at the house.

Immediately, my senses switch to high alert, and I find myself reaching out from within, trying to discern the shape and feel of the intruder's spirit. He's too far away though, and Kincaid lays a hand on mine, making me start.

"He's one of mine," he explains before stepping out of the car, making the whole thing jar and shake with the absence of his weight.

"Darius." Kincaid nods in greeting. "What is it?"

I straighten Kincaid's jacket over my torn shirt, fastening the two bronze clasps to hold it shut. It does little to cover the swell of my breasts or the slender pane of my stomach, but at least my nipples are covered. It would have to do.

It wasn't as if anyone here would judge me. Most of the Diablim women I'd seen were half naked even on a chilly day in Elisium.

"We found Zak," the Diablim man called Darius tells Kincaid, eyeing me warily as I approach. He has eyes that are all black from edge to edge, and a strange bird-like quality to his features that's somehow both bewitching and unnerving.

"Good."

Darius looks between Kincaid and me, and I get the sense he's waiting for me to leave. I move away, but Kincaid pulls me back, keeping me rooted to his side.

Taking his master's cue, Darius continues. "Would you like to deal with him yourself, my lord, or would you have us deal with him for you?"

"I'll deal with it, but it will have to wait. I have other matters to attend to."

"Anything I can assist with?"

Kincaid's lips purse as he considers. "There's a house in Infernum I need to locate. Reach out to our contacts there and have them find it. A blue house with a rose garden in front. It would be somewhere on the outskirts of the city. Tell them not to get too close if they find it. The one inhabiting it will know I'm coming if she senses something amiss."

Darius' eyes narrow, but he doesn't ask any further questions. "I'll have the intel for you within seventy-two hours."

"You have forty-eight."

Darius departs, and Kincaid and I go inside.

"How many Diablim do you have under your command?"

"Taking her to The Freakshow, Kincaid?" a familiar voice demands, and I whirl to find Tori storming toward us from the kitchen with Artemis on her heels. "What the hell were you thinking?"

"*Tori,*" Kincaid grits out. "Always a pleasure."

"S-Sorry," Artemis stutters. "She just kinda barged in."

Kincaid's eyes spark with annoyance. "She has a tendency to do that."

Tori rolls her violet eyes at him and comes to embrace me, but stops just shy of wrapping her arms around me, assessing me like a hawk instead. She raises a brow as she pulls a stray leaf from my hair and takes in what I'm wearing. Then her lips part and she gapes at Kincaid.

I can feel the evidence of what Kincaid and I did out in the woods written in bold print all over my body. I wriggle under Tori's gaze as she reads it all, looking a little sick after a minute.

"You okay, love?"

"I'm fine," I reply, voice cracking with embarrassment.

"You seem different."

Could be that I've been touched by a man—a demon man—*in that way* for the first time in my life. Could also be the fact that I just killed two Diablim.

Maybe both.

Maybe neither.

I probably just need a bath.

"Why are you here, Tori?" Kincaid grouses, pinching the bridge of his nose.

"Did you not say I was welcome to be here?" she asks with a challenge in her eyes and a note of impatience in her tone. I want to be her when I grow up.

For whatever insane reason, she isn't afraid of Kincaid like everyone else in this devil's playground. She just doesn't give a flying fuck about his status or what it should demand from a constituent like herself.

"You're testing my patience," Kincaid warns, and she *snickers* at him.

I clasp my hand tightly into Kincaid's, getting seriously worried he'll reduce her to a pile of blood and ash at our feet if she keeps going. Kincaid meets my worried gaze with an amused one, and I settle, knowing somehow from that look alone that he has no malintent toward her. No matter how insufferable she can be.

"I came to warn you," she says. "And to check on Paige, but I can see you're taking *very* good care of her."

I wish I could disappear.

"Get to the point, Tor."

"There's talk among the Nephilim. They're getting curious, Kincaid. *Too curious.*"

"We know."

"There's something else; Carver isn't in his hole."

Both Kincaid and Artemis visibly blanche, and I try not to do the same, making a mental note to make Kincaid explain to me exactly who this Carver is and what he wants with me.

"I didn't believe it myself, so I went to check. Carver hasn't left his hole in a decade, but he wasn't there. He can't leave Elisium so… he has to be in the city."

"I should have dealt with him at the start," Kincaid mutters to himself, searching the marble tile at his feet as though an answer is hidden in the reflection.

"Probably." Tori shrugs. "Just thought you should know."

"I've had my men watching his lair for the last few days. *Worthless ingrates.* If you ever want a job that pays better than selling knickknacks—"

"I happen to *like* selling my knickknacks, *thank you very much.*"

Kincaid's lips lift in the ghost of a smile, and for the first time, I wonder if they have ever had a relationship. It would explain why Tori is so at ease with him, and why he doesn't cut her down for speaking to him the way she does.

I'm surprised at the way the thought affects me. Worries me.

I consider Tori in a new light. An admittedly *greener* one.

She's beautiful. The most beautiful being I've encountered in Elisium aside from Kincaid and maybe Dantalion and that angel who'd been at the Midnight court. A vein twitches in my temple and Tori cocks her head at me, reminding me to keep my emotions from my face.

"If he gives you a hard time, you know where to find me. You're welcome on my couch anytime."

"Thanks, Tori," I say with an impish grin, jealousy melting into guilt when she embraces me, leaving a light kiss on my right cheek.

"I'll let you know if I hear anything else," she calls with a wave of her hand as she leaves. "Take care of our girl, Kincaid. I'll be holding you personally responsible if anything happens to her."

I snack on one of the bagels Tori brought, not bothering to toast or butter it first, finding I'm absolutely ravenous.

Artemis excuses himself to go back to bed once Tori left, and even though I think it may help him sleep at night to know the Old Crones were dead, I can't bring myself to tell him. Not because I regret it, but because I worry he might judge me for *not* having an ounce of remorse.

Aren't you supposed to *feel* something when you take a life, even if it's for the greater good? Shouldn't I feel ill? Racked by guilt. Feel like my hands would always be stained a vivid blood red? That's how it is in the movies. That's how it is in the books.

Instead, I feel a sick sort of satisfaction. A satisfaction that led to almost losing my virginity on a dirty patch of forest to a demon.

I take another monster-sized bite of the bagel and sigh.

"What are you thinking about?" I ask Kincaid, needing a distraction from my own thoughts. He's been quiet since Tori left, sitting stoically at the table with a glass of amber liquid that he hasn't touched in his hands. Instead, he swirls the liquid, watching it shimmer against the beveled edges of the glass.

"Hmm?"

"Are you going to tell me who Carver is?"

He puts the glass to his lips and tips the contents down his throat, rising to pour another.

"Can I try some?"

He pauses but then draws out another glass and tips a miniscule amount of the liquor into it, filling his about halfway. "You won't like it."

I take the proffered cup and sniff, almost choking on the acrid bouquet. Beneath the tang of alcohol there is a familiar scent. Sandalwood and smoke.

It reminds me of Kincaid, and I take a sip. Once you get past the harshness, it's actually not bad. I take another sip, and Kincaid seems suspicious, but says nothing, putting himself on the edge of the table.

"I need to ask something of you, *Na'vazēm.*"

I think I may already know what it is, but I ask anyway. "What?"

He reaches over to brush his fingers through my hair, loosening more debris from the long colorful locks. I flush.

"I need you to try to speak with Malphas again. Or perhaps, to attempt to commune with Dantalion."

The warmth of the liquor in my belly turns rapidly to a chill, and I squirm in my seat. I knew it was only a matter of time until he asked. I guess I hoped he would find what he needed to know elsewhere, and then he wouldn't need to.

"You want me to use the Scepter again."

It's not a question, but still I need him to confirm it, just so I know exactly what his expectations are. I promised him my cooperation—to follow *all* of his commands until the end of forty days. I wish I could hold on to the belief that things have changed enough between us that he won't hurt me if I refuse, but I can't.

I'm still his property. He's still one of the seven lords of Hell.

We have a bargain.

Whatever else we are, it won't be enough to erase any of that.

"Yes. I think that's the only way."

"I understand."

I finish my glass and push it onto the table, snatching his from his fingers and standing, leaving my half-eaten bagel discarded on the table. My reflection stares back at me from the water-streaked windowpane in the dining room. Scrawny and caged in. It's no wonder I've barely managed to put on more than a few pounds since I've been here, there's always something curbing my appetite. Making my belly sour.

"I hope you also understand that I wouldn't ask it of you unless I had another option."

He heaves a long breath, and I hear the creak of ancient wood as he rises behind me. Feel the heat of his body as he nears until the reflection of him appears in the darkened panes of glass. A devil above my shoulder.

"I must find out how they were killed. I've exhausted every other option. This is all that's left. As impossible as it should be, if you can see then—speak to them—it may be the only way to stop whatever it is that's causing it."

My jaw aches from clenching, and I have to work to loosen my grip on the glass in my hand for fear of shattering it.

The sharp image of Dantalion dying without having seen a single thing to cause it sends my pulse fluttering beneath my breastbone. Any minute. Any day. That could be Kincaid.

He could drop dead right now and there would be no way for me to stop it. I close my eyes and my shoulders sag. "I'll do it."

Of course, I would. Did I have any other option?

His light touch on my arms sends a different sort of tremor through me and I bristle, gooseflesh rising on my arms. He lays a soft kiss on the base of my neck and a breath whistles in through my teeth before I turn to look into his eyes.

"When?"

"Once we have Devereaux. I want her with you in case anything should happen."

"Can't she do it?"

Kincaid's expression shifts, darkening. "She's one of the most powerful Necromancers to ever live, and she has never missed an opportunity to remind me that I have no soul. I do not think she will be able to wield the Scepter as you can. I do not think she will be able to contact my brothers."

...then why can I?

I can see the question mirrored in his gaze just as much as I'm certain he can see it in mine. Neither of us have the answer.

"Two days then?" I press, remembering that Kincaid only gave his henchmen forty-eight hours to find the location of Deveraux's little blue house. I have to assume Kincaid won't want to waste time.

"I'll have to go to Infernum myself to convince her to come."

He grimaces.

"Are you going to leave me here?"

He takes the liquor back from me and gulps some down, licking the rim of the glass. He doesn't answer for so long that I think he hasn't heard me, but then he shakes his head, dark hair falling low to cover his eyes.

"I can't," he relents. "I should, but with the Carver loose in the city...demon-bond or not, I won't risk leaving you."

My upper lip curls at the reminder. "Where is Casper, anyway?"

I strain my ears, listening for his little bell, but hear nothing. "Upstairs in your room. I believe Artemis locked him inside."

A small laugh balloons in my throat. Sounds like something Artemis would do.

"So, how do we get to Infernum? The Underbridge?"

I wouldn't say as much, but I seriously doubt we'll be able to escape notice and travel hundreds of miles undetected to get there. Though the idea of seeing so much of the world excites me beyond words.

"No. We'll use the staff."

"The staff? The one that takes us to Hell?"

Suddenly staying behind doesn't seem like such a bad idea. I'm sure I'll be fine with Casper and Artemis. Yeah. No need to take me with him.

"It can also transport between Fallen Cities. Well… the ones occupied by one of the seven lords. We are part of Hell, just as an angel is part of Heaven." He finishes the drink. "The pull of my brothers is just as strong as the pull of our kingdom."

My heart bleeds for him, but before I have a chance to say a word or to comfort him, the grief in his gaze vanishes. "We'll have to pay a visit to Belial."

"Your brother?"

"Hmm." He nods, and I don't like the way his face looks. Pinched. His body coiled like a serpent, anticipating attack. "Do not speak to him, *Na'vazēm.* Do not even look at him. He's a creature of whim, and he rules his city in a much *different* way."

I've heard of Infernum. Of the city inhabited by a large subsect of salamanders and other fire-born creatures of the dark. They say it smolders so persistently that the air for miles around smells of sulfur and the historical temperatures have risen by several degrees.

Lacey Lewis has said that any human who's dared come near to it is never seen again.

No one knows what it looks like inside, either. Even drones can't capture clear images for all the steam and smoke.

I FIND MYSELF EQUAL PARTS EXHILARATED AND TERRIFIED to see what lies within the barriers of runed black salt and the Mississippi River that cage in what used to be New Orleans.

11

The days pass in a blur, and I get more and more restless every minute. Artemis found an old chess board in the basement and we've spent the last two evenings playing well into the night since sleep is firmly *off* the table.

What's driving me to the edge of madness isn't even that we're nearing the tail end of the forty-eight-hour deadline and will have to go to Infernum. No, it's that Kincaid hasn't touched me since that night at The Freakshow.

I'd been so frazzled after our conversation in the dining room that all I wanted was some solitude to think it through. Not just what happened that night, but Carver, Lady Devereaux, and the prospect of meeting another lord of the underworld.

Maybe that was the mistake, going to close myself in my room with Casper and stare at the ceiling for hours until sleep finally took me near dawn. I didn't know what the hell I was supposed to do in this situation.

Did I just invite myself into his bed? Did I wait for him to make another move—like a flower that only blooms in certain slants of light? Just remain shuttered up and dead to all the world unless he touched me? *Ugh.*

I would *not* be that.

Not for anyone, even if he does make my heart splutter and my toes curl every time he speaks.

"Checkmate," Artemis says, though with less of his usual mirth after defeating me. I was still learning to play, so a win on my part was rare. "How did you not see that coming? I couldn't have made it more obvious. You could have blocked me at least four times."

I blink, seeing my mistakes. "Right."

"Are you okay?"

"Fine."

"Trouble in paradise?"

"Artemis, I swear to God if you don't shut up—"

"Don't swear to Him. He doesn't care."

It's such an odd thing to say that I forget what had me so annoyed for a second and analyze the sudden hardness around his light brown eyes.

"Are *you* okay?"

He begins putting away the pieces, scooching out of the way when Casper strolls into the room and walks right over the board, knocking what remains of the still-standing pieces to their backs.

We have a sort of understanding, this demon and me. I had a stern chat with it the other night. I promised not to roast it over a pit until it released my soul in exchange for a lifetime of head pats. It only meowed plaintively at me, but I took that to mean it agreed.

I couldn't stay away from the thing, anyhow. Now that I understood the bond between us a little better, it was easy to figure out why. With a part of my own soul now living inside the creature—a piece that was sliced off the moment I named him, he became a sort of extension of myself. I couldn't keep him away from me any better than I could run from my own shadow.

"I'm not the one pining after a demon lord like a lovesick looney."

I guffaw at him. "That is not true."

He smirks. "Isn't it?"

"You think I'm acting crazy?" I ask a few moments later, once Casper is curled up on my pillows and all the chess pieces are neatly put away.

Artemis shrugs.

"I like him," I admit in a whisper, the words spilling out. I think they've been trying to be set free for a while. "More than I should."

"He's all right," Artemis agrees. "Still a psychopath, but not the worst kind I've ever met."

After the silence stretches on a little longer between

us, I think of some other direction to turn the conversation, not wanting him to leave just yet. It's barely midnight, and I'll be up for hours still. Better with company, even if he just teases me the whole damn time. I've spent enough of my life alone.

Though before I can blurt the first thing that comes to mind, Artemis sits up straighter and lifts his head. "I think you should probably talk to him about it."

"Huh?"

"Look," he says. "After what you did for me, I'm going to be honest with you because I think I owe you that."

I don't like where this is going.

"I'm not an expert or anything, but I've spent enough time here in Elisium that I think maybe I know a bit more about the folk that live here than you do."

"Just spit it out."

He flicks his hair away from his face and chews the inside of his lips. "He's a demon. Like, one of *the* demons. The original seven. Whatever it is you think you feel for him, I don't think it's really a good idea to, like, you know..."

No, I really don't, but the shimmer of fury zaps in the air and it takes all of my restraint not to snap at him. I can't, not when I know that whatever he's trying to say, he is right. It hurts too much to admit it.

"You're pretty." Art shrugs. "He's, I dunno, lonely, maybe?"

"So you think he's using me, is that it?"

He holds his hands up, falling back. "I don't know, Paige. I'm just saying I wouldn't—"

"Well I didn't ask for your opinion."

He gets up and snorts. "Sorry I said anything," he says snidely and then leaves, shutting the door behind him.

"This is some bullshit, Cas," I say to the sleeping cat on my bed and shove the chessboard away. "What is wrong with me?"

Why the hell did I care?

I was so stupid to think that…

What did I think?

I let my head fall into my hands and curl my knees into my chest, trying to erase the intrusive thoughts from my skull. I knock my head against my knees, and when they still remain, I do it again, harder.

Grit my teeth.

Harder.

Once more.

"Paige," the roar out in the hall sends tremors down my spine, and I scramble to my feet before he barges inside. He scans the room for a threat, his calculating stare landing on me, perplexed.

Startled, I remembered how he can feel my emotions. It isn't just desire, though I'm coming to understand that is his favorite one—the one he likes to wield against people. But he could also sense my shame at Ford's house.

And whatever nameless thing I feel now…

Perhaps he knows what it is.

"Is it time to go?" I ask, entirely dismissing his clear apprehension and evicting whatever remains of my frustration from my head with a quick count to three.

He blinks at me, taken aback, and straightens. I don't miss how his gaze passes over my forehead, where I'm sure there is an angry red mark at best, and some minor bruising at worst. With my new healing speed, though, it will be gone within a few minutes, leaving him to wonder if it'd been there at all.

The violent urge to bend my fingers to snapping behind my back sends uneasy ripples through my stomach. For a moment, I'm afraid I might be sick, but then the moment passes and Kincaid holds the door open.

"I have the location," Kincaid says. "I was going to wait until morning—"

"No need. I can't sleep."

His lips press together. "You'll want to change."

I glance down at the single pair of stretchy pants I'd managed to find in that godawful store Kincaid took me to and the wooly socks on my feet. It's cold in the mansion at night and I usually have to double up socks to sleep and wear a sweater under my weighted blanket.

"Too hot there?" I guess, leaning on my minimal knowledge.

Kincaid nods, looking more uncomfortable than I've ever seen him. "I'll wait outside."

"No need."

I strip down to my panties on the spot, tossing my warm sweater and pants on the bed to dig a denim skirt and too-tight black t-shirt out of the dresser. I've been washing the clothing myself in the bathroom sink and it shows. Though I haven't worn the skirt yet, leaving it to look clean, pressed, and new, the shirt is a favorite of mine, and so it has stiff crinkles from where it was folded and smells faintly of the soap I found in the bathroom.

It itches a little.

I don't look to see if Kincaid watches me as I dress, but only because I don't have to. I can feel his stare. It brings a light flush to my cheeks, but I don't let the feeling fester, replacing it with false confidence instead.

Artemis may be right, but I don't have to give Kincaid what he wants from me. If he truly only wants to use me as a plaything to pass the time, then I can simply deny him. Problem solved.

I would just *not* let myself feel anything more for him and whatever feelings I still had would wane over time.

In the meantime, though, I can punish him a little.

"Are you…are you trying to *tease* me?"

Though, I didn't quite expect to be called out on it…

"No," I tell him, tugging the t-shirt over my bare breasts, sealing off my emotions from his ability to read them the best I can. "I'm just doing my best not to be a *prude*."

I give myself a mental smack and find myself buried under layers of insanity caused by this devil of a man standing in front of me. Dust her off, pick her up.

Get your shit together, Paige.

Kincaid seals his lips against a smile that makes me want to rage and sweeps an arm toward my bedroom door. "Very well, *Na'vazēm.* Shall we go?"

12

I tuck close into Kincaid's side as he lifts the staff above the marble floor in the entryway, fisting my fingers in the soft fabric of his shirt. "Don't let go," he says, and I squeeze my eyes shut and bite down.

The floor falls out from under us, and I don't dare open my eyes as we hurtle through time and space. A strange wind kicks up my hair and finds its way up my skirt. All I can smell is hickory and smoke, my face buried entirely in Kincaid's side. His arm tightens around my middle as we are deposited onto solid ground again, keeping me from plummeting to my face on the pavement.

A shout follows and then the whispers that seem to follow Kincaid everywhere rise. My stomach roils, but I gulp down the nausea and force myself to stand erect, my knees threatening to give out. A sulfuric odor permeates the air and Kincaid was right about the heat.

Already a lick of sweat forms on my brow, and I blink into the hazy air, trying to find my bearings.

"Do you need a moment?" Kincaid asks, still gripping me around the middle while he stares at the curious Diablim onlookers with enough dangerous intent that they all begin to scatter.

I shake my head. "No, I'll be fine. Just need to catch my breath."

He loosens his hold, and I test my balance, finding I'm all right to stand on my own.

"You get used to it," he tells me and I bark a laugh, holding a hand to my still-roiling belly.

"I hope I never need to."

I can feel his smiling eyes on me as I take in our surroundings, going slack-jawed as I do.

Directly in front of us is a building that almost looks like a castle, but the white facade and tall arched windows give away what it truly is—or *was*.

A cathedral.

"Is this…"

"The Infernum court," he replies in answer to my unasked question. "Belial has always had a dark sense of humor."

I spin, taking in a market down the way and several other old buildings. Diablim mill about, sneaking glances our way as they shop and drink in the square.

"He'll know I've arrived by now," he adds. "We should go inside."

I follow closely at Kincaid's right side, keeping myself as inconspicuous and out of view as I can—just like he told me to.

Tall wooden doors with iron hinges open before us, as though the building itself knew we were coming, ushering us into a lair of chaos.

A HAUNTING SONG OF JAZZ VIOLIN AND DRUM accompanies lusty whispered vocals that make my skin bristle and my core tighten. Diablim writhe to the sway and pulse of the music, many of them entirely naked, their faces slack and eyes heavy.

These Diablim pay no heed to us as we enter, and the heavy doors sweep shut behind us. Vaulted cathedral ceilings dome us in forty feet above, Latin inscriptions in the beam work have been scratched out and candles flicker in old wrought iron chandeliers. There are two levels, and from down here I can see Diablim are dancing and feasting in the upper level, too, leaning down to watch those below with disinterested stares.

A Diablim swirls into my path, a woman with breasts the size of melons and a waist so tiny it's a wonder she doesn't snap in half from the weight of them. On her palm is a black tray with a mirrored surface. Atop it sit little piles of a fine silver powder. It shimmers like glitter in the flickering lights.

Kincaid waves her off, and she goes, offering the tray instead to another Diablim. He lifts a short stick and snorts the powder into his nose violently, his body convulsing as the substance enters his system.

I gape at them all, unsure what to make of what I'm seeing, until Kincaid presses a hand to my lower back, urging me forward to a dais.

Headless statues hide in the crooks of a massive stone structure and in the center, sitting high above the din below, is a man who looks like he could be the devil himself. He has eyes like fire and deep brown hair that waves down past his chin. He's clad in black robes with a belt of shining gold. Barefoot and bare chested. A thin gold circlet on his crown.

"Brother!"

"Belial," Kincaid replies with a light in his eyes like I've never seen in him before. "Good to see you."

I keep my head down as well as I can as Kincaid weaves through the throng of intoxicated Diablim, making his way to his brother's makeshift throne.

Belial descends and they embrace fiercely, but the smile Belial gives Kincaid makes my insides knot. It's warm enough, but paired with the hellish pits of his eyes, only serves to make him look psychotic.

Like a smile he might give someone before gleefully gutting them and using their entrails as adornment for his hall.

"And this must be the Diablim I've heard so much about."

When Belial turns his attention to me, I'm not prepared. My foot slips on the stone step, and I fall back, knocking into a scalding hot naked body. She screeches as a black tray flies out of her hand, toppling the glittering silver contents so it falls like rain all over me.

I push off from her, cringing when I feel soft breast tissue and a pebbled nipple under my fingers. I choke on the woody taste in my mouth and try my best to wipe it from my face, feeling the sting of it in my nostrils.

"Yes," Kincaid says, clearing his throat as I pick my way back to his side, absolutely sure that my entire face is tomato red and I'm about to die of embarrassment. "This is Paige. Paige, my brother Belial, Lord of the Underworld and warden of Infernum."

I want desperately to spit the vile taste from my mouth, but I don't dare, swallowing it down instead. I catch Kincaid giving me a strange look as his brother steps down to greet me. I can't be sure, but I think he's afraid.

And it makes a hollow pit form in my stomach.

"A pretty thing, isn't she?" Belial says, putting his face close enough that I can feel the whisper of his breath on my cheek.

So much for keeping out of his notice.

"So, girl, what do you think of Infernum?"

"It's...um...hot?"

Belial arches back with a roar of laughter, his hand

pressed against the muscles of his abdomen. I notice golden rings adorn each of his fingers; two are caked with flakey crimson.

"Not a very witty one, is she?" he says, swiping at a tear before leveling the full weight of his stare on me once more.

I flinch when he reaches out, his fingers lightning quick, like the strike of a snake. He flicks his fingers over my cheek, swiping some of the remaining powder from my skin before sticking the two digits into his mouth.

He bites his lower lip when he withdraws them and shivers with delight. "Shall we share her, Brother? Like we used to?"

My face heats again, and I don't breathe until Kincaid speaks and Belial moves away, letting my breath out in a gush of hot air.

"I'm afraid not."

"Pity," Belial pouts. "She smells like a virgin."

A thick vein in Kincaid's neck pulses, betraying his fury, but he finds the will to offer his brother a smile. "There's much we should discuss, but I'm here on an errand."

Belial puts a hand to his chest as though his brother's words wound him. "You haven't come to partake in the glorious debauchery of my court, Asmodeus? Is that not reason enough to visit? You offend me."

I can't be certain, but I think, *I hope,* Belial is joking. I can't imagine what a demon like him would do if he felt truly offended. I want to giggle at the absurdity of the images in my head. Of a distraught Belial tossing around headless Diablim as though they were toys.

I shudder, and the muscles that've been tense in my shoulders for weeks begin to tingle. The mild pain and discomfort ebbs away, being replaced by something soothing and warm.

All of my thoughts have a soft edge to them, a distant quality that makes me wonder if I'm dreaming. I can hear my own heartbeat thundering like the hooves of a galloping racehorse in my chest. The sound drowns out most all the others in the room.

As though from very far away, Belial and Kincaid continue their conversation. Yellow eyes flit my way every few seconds and I want to rub at the knot of flesh between them. Tell him not to worry.

My head is light, and when a Diablim brushes up against my back it's like being touched by an angel. The woman with bright eyes and tattoos covering her bald head beckons me to dance and I long to go, but Kincaid told me I must stay here. I mustn't leave his side.

I pull back when she tugs on my arm again, and she snaps at me with pointed teeth. There's a silvery gleam coating her fangs, stuck to the skin just beneath her nostrils.

The powder.

The drug.

A moment of clarity kickstarted by fear makes my

pulse thunder anew. I ingested it. That's why I feel strange. I ingested the drug.

And its effects are only just beginning. I find Kincaid, my chest heaving, and try to implore him with a look alone that I need to leave. The tingling that began in my shoulders has spread down my arms, and I can't feel my fingers.

I'm swaying, and I'm not sure when it started. Not sure how to make it stop.

"I'll return in an hour and we can talk. I'll take the car."

Belial leaves Kincaid to slouch back onto his makeshift throne. He waves a beautiful girl with a bright violet hued aura to his side and roughly tugs her into his lap. She grins as he wraps his slender fingers around her throat, grinding her hips into his lap. "Very well, *Brother*. I expect you'll have some knowledge of where my vanished kin have gone."

He says this like a threat and an almost irresistible urge to rip his soul from his bones overtakes me. How dare he threaten Kincaid. Only my demon's gentle touch as he wraps an arm around my shoulders stops me from trying.

"That is what we are trying to find out."

Belial flicks his wrist in dismissal and a gush of outside air rushes into the desecrated cathedral as the tall doors swing open. It's all I can do to stay on my feet as Kincaid rushes us out.

☙ 13 ❧

We veer into an alley half a block down from the cathedral and Kincaid presses me up against the wall, jerking my chin up. He stares into me, assessing, and then his gaze sweeps over the rest of my face and body.

"How much did you ingest?"

"What is it?" I ask, my voice coming out slow. Oozing like molasses.

Kincaid releases me, and I let my head droop, tilting my neck to look up at him from beneath the safety of my lashes. They're so long that I can see the edges of them at this angle. I never noticed that before.

"Angel's tears."

"What!"

He curses in another language and continues dragging me down the narrow alleyway, kicking debris out of the way as we go. "Not *actual* angel's tears. It's

Belial's blasphemous name for his creation. I have no idea what's in it. It's a guarded secret so he can be the only supplier."

Huh.

"How much did you ingest?" he repeats, this time in a snarl that makes me want to pull away.

"I don't know," I say on a laugh, not sure what's funny. Nothing, I suppose. And everything. "Not a lot. *Just enough*, I think."

"I should take you back."

"No!"

This time, I do pull against his hold, but not to get away, to make him stop. To bring him closer. "Don't leave me there, Kincaid. I have to stay with you."

I manage to bite off the rest of what I'd been about to say, knowing he'd only laugh if I told him it was because I needed to protect him. I may be the only person who has any hope of somehow putting his soul back in his body if what happened to Dantalion and Malphas happens to him.

"You think I want to?" he spits with a glare.

I'm not sure why, but suddenly, I want to cry. My eyes burn. "I didn't *mean* to," I choke, the sadness suddenly evaporating as a new emotion takes its place. "Don't be such an *asshole*."

His nostrils flare, but he says nothing in reply, just jerks his chin to the edge of the alley, where a sleek black car is parked. I follow wordlessly, shouldering past him to open my own door when he tries to do it for me. "I think I can open my own door," I snap, sliding into the low leather seat.

It's nothing like any of Kincaid's cars. His are all roomy and speak of history—character. This is a modern beast of LED lights and muted black leather and chrome.

The seat slides against my slippery skin, eliciting a lascivious response that makes me press my thighs together and bite my tongue. I can't remember what I was so angry about when Kincaid slides into the car next to me. I lick my lips as he starts the engine, and the purr of it vibrating up through my core makes me want to moan.

"Paige," Kincaid warns, "*Please.*"

I remember that I'm supposed to be good, and I fold my hands into my lap, squeezing them tight together to keep them from reaching out to touch him.

Kincaid peels the car out from the side of the street, forcing Diablim in the roadway to flee, screeching and calling after him. I'm sucked back into my seat and I laugh at the sensation. My stomach left eight blocks back in the blink of an eye.

On a whim, I roll down the window and a blast of hot air gushes into the car, battering my face. I press into it, enjoying how it rushes over my skin.

INFERNUM PASSES BY IN A BLUR AS KINCAID SPEEDS through the streets, not paying heed to any traffic signs or the fact that there are Diablim in the road. He drives around them and any obstacles in our path, making my body jerk back and forth in the seat. It's what I imagine a carnival ride to feel like.

I wonder if Kincaid will take me back to The Freakshow so I can ride the great metal contraptions there, but I don't ask him. Speaking would ruin this feeling of light and blissful joy, I just know it. And I want to keep it for as long as I can.

When I open my eyes, it's to flashes of barren darkness and then landscapes of fire. Horrific things and beautiful things. Things I have to question whether are real or simply vivid hallucinations brought on by the Angel's Tears.

When the flutter in my rib cage begins to slow and I fall against the seat once more, I think it's safe to talk. The moment of bliss is already ebbing anyhow.

"Where are we going again?"

"Out near the Bayou. Lady Devereaux lives at the edge of the lagoon."

Right. Lady Devereaux. The Necromancer.

Which, apparently, I am not.

What's the point of this again? I sigh. Who cares.

A few minutes later, Kincaid slows the car and we continue at a crawl over busted pavement and dirt, bumping along a dark road hedged in by walls of viridian green on both sides.

There's a distinct tug inside my chest and I gasp,

thinking my heart has found a way to leap out with all its incessant pounding. Until I feel it again.

"She knows we're coming," I say on a breath, my words so low they are almost lost to the breeze rushing through the cabin of the car. I'm not sure how, but I can tell it's her.

She's feeling me out. Drawing me in. The feel of her feeling me is a curious one. Lady Devereaux has extended an invitation. "She's inviting us to come in."

Kincaid looks at me like I've grown another head when I throw an arm out and shout at him. "Stop. You've passed it. It's through there."

I point at the wall of gnarled and side-bending trees covered in vines like little bushy skirts around their middles. There's a gap in them, but it's hard to see because of the angle. "There. We need to go that way."

I jump out, unperturbed when my feet squish into a muddy puddle and I have to lift them out. The sucking sounds make me grin.

"*Na'vazēm,* wait."

"Come on, slow poke. She doesn't like to be kept waiting."

Kincaid catches up a moment later, leaving the car idling behind us. He grunts something unintelligible and falls into stride next to me.

Following the Necromancer's pull, I lead us back out from a mossy trail and onto more solid ground, following a maze-like path through the foggy trees. We come upon it after a few more turns, and I have to ask how Kincaid's henchmen were able to find the place, because without Lady Devereaux's help, I doubt I ever would've.

Her pretty blue house is propped up by a platform on stilts, making it look as though it's got legs of its own and can move at will. Its twin windows in the front, lashed with red roses, and a matching front door could be eyes and a mouth.

I imagine the white blinds lifting. The eyes opening. And the mouth swallowing us up. I wonder what we taste like.

The stairs creak as we ascend them, and I'm disappointed when the door opens, revealing a very ordinary interior and not the stomach of a monstrous walking house-beast. Too bad.

Not so ordinary, though, is the woman who turns away from the door as swiftly as she opened it, leaving us to stand unattended on her stoop.

"Well, get inside if you must," she calls, her voice a slightly hoarse utterance of rushed speech.

Kincaid goes in first and I follow him, feeling heavy as I pass over the threshold, like I've just walked into a wall of thick air and my legs have to wade through it to keep me moving forward.

It's spirit energy, I realize, feeling the rap of phantom fingers on the doors to my mind.

The woman with long silvery hair to match her reflective eyes hobbles to a plush pink armchair and plops herself into it, taking up a ball of yarn and knitting needles from a basket beside her.

I giggle.

"Something funny, girl?" she snaps at me, and I shut my trap, clasping my hands together. The picture of composure, just like Kincaid asked. It's easier now. I think the drug is starting to wear off, or maybe the weight of the energy in this house is keeping it held back. Either way, I'm grateful for the reprieve of semi-clear thoughts.

...but also a little hungry for the bliss of the angel's tears to return.

"Asmodeus," the old woman says, drawing out his name as her needles click and clack against one another, forming something new. "To what do I owe this pleasure?"

"I'm calling in my favor."

"Are you, now?"

Her reflective eyes find mine, and I jerk forward as she tugs at me from the inside out, nearly falling to my knees. "For this one, I assume?"

He nods gravely, eyes glimmering with warning until the woman releases her hold on my soul and I gasp in a breath.

"She needs training. Her ability is out of control. You will help her learn to wield it. To control it."

"I will, will I?"

"Don't test me, Devereaux."

She sets down her knitting and waves me forward

with two crooked fingers. She looks like she's a hundred years old.

I look to Kincaid for guidance, and he gestures for me to do as she asks, so I do. Clenching my fists, I cross the carpeted and rugged floor and stand before her in her worn pink chair. She grips me by the wrist, and I feel an invasive prickle roll up through my arm.

It searches, gaining speed as she feels out the edges of my soul. It's an awful feeling and I cringe, making a mental note to apologize to Artemis for using him as practice.

"You're a strange one," she says when she lets go and I clutch my wrist to my chest, rubbing out the ghost of her touch. "Not a Necromancer. Not as I am, anyhow. But a spirit-worker all the same."

"Can you help her?"

"You should kill her," Lady Deveraux replies to Kincaid, and the sweat chills on my body. "Her power is too great, Asmodeus. I don't know what she is, but untrained, she's a danger to everyone around her."

"That isn't an option."

The necromancer grimaces; her eyes, the mirror image of mine, narrow to slits.

"Are you saying you can't do it?" Kincaid challenges her.

She huffs. "I'm old, Asmodeus. Retired."

"But not dead."

"Not yet."

She purses her lips, accentuating all of her wrinkles.

"You'll consider our debt settled when I'm through with her?"

"I will."

She shakes her head, eyeing me up and down as she does. "All right. I'll do it."

Kincaid extends his hand to her, and with a curl in her lip, she takes it, sealing the deal.

"I'll be using a priceless favor to export you to Elisium. I'll expect you to be ready at dawn."

"Yes, yes," Lady Devereaux chuffs. "As you say."

"If you aren't here," he begins to warn, and she looks at him like he may be the stupidest lad she's ever laid eyes on.

"Are you daft? I said I'd do it, so I will and that's that. Now, if you'll excuse me I'd like to finish my knitting."

Once back outside, Kincaid gives my hand a squeeze.

"Is she always so…"

I couldn't think of the right word.

"Bitter?" he offers.

I nod.

"No," he replies and I heave a sigh of relief until he tips his head down to stare at me with mischief in his eyes. "She's usually much worse."

14

"What happened to you?"

I sit on the edge of my bed, my aching head resting in my hands. Palm pressing into my eye-sockets to numb the discomfort.

"Go away, Artemis," I moan, shivering against a cool sweat breaking out over my chest.

If this is a hangover, I'm *never* drinking or touching any form of drug *ever* again. It's atrocious.

Artemis sniffs, and I hear his footsteps pause a few feet away. "Why do you smell like a roast pigeon?"

I really don't want to know how he knows what that smells like. Blindly, I reach out a hand to try to shove him off, but he's just out of reach. "Make yourself useful and get me some water."

"I can do that, but first I've been ordered to tell you by a very rude old woman that you need to come downstairs. She said she doesn't like to be kept waiting."

"Please tell me you're kidding."

"Nope," he says, lips popping. "She got here hours ago. Moved in down the hall. Master Kincaid said to stay out of her way. That she was here to train you."

"What time is it?"

"Almost three?"

"In the morning?"

With the heavy blanket I threw over the window, it's impossible to tell the time, but I know I'm only giving myself false hope.

"Considering you got home at four in the morning…"

"Will you just," I wave him over, "do your thing, please. My head feels like it's splitting in two."

Artemis rests his hands on the back of my head, and I tremble as a seeking warmth radiates down my spine, numbing some of the pain. The throbbing behind my eyes dulls to a barely noticeable thudding and when I open my eyes for the second time this morning, they don't burn quite as much.

"Thank you," I murmur. "And I'm sorry about last night. I was…I don't know what I was."

"Sexually frustrated?"

"Art."

"Fine. I'll stop. You just make it so easy to get under your skin."

"If I ever decide I want kids, talk me out of it, okay?"

Artemis laughs and helps me up, squinting at the state of me. I'm afraid to ask, but it turns out I don't have to. He's perfectly happy to tell me exactly what he sees. The little shit.

"You look like you got run over by a truck."

"Thanks. That's sweet."

"And I think there's a bird's nest in the back of your head."

"*Out.* Get out before I eat your soul, you little heathen."

He rushes away with a chuckle and calls back, "That old lady said she's going to drag you down there if you don't come on your own! I'd hurry if I were you. She doesn't seem like the type to mess around."

No, she certainly didn't.

I take a moment to crack my stiff neck and stretch out my legs before padding to the bathroom. After the luxurious bath in Kincaid's tub last week, washing my usual way, in three inches of water on the shower floor has been a sad occurrence.

If I had the gall, I'd just ask to use his bathroom, but other than that first night, he seems to be entirely fine with me sleeping in my own room. It's impossible not to wonder what changed, but I try to put that out of my mind as I lather soap through my hair and scrub left-over dirt from beneath my fingernails.

As clean as I'll be getting, I drain the gray-tinted water and step out, quickly turning on the shower head and removing my arm to rinse away the dirt residue from the shower floor before quickly turning it off. My heart jackhammering in my chest and a ball forming in my throat.

I glare at the showerhead, making the decision to defeat the metal foe next time.

A showerhead is *not* the hose. I am *not* at Ford's house anymore.

"Next time," I whisper, pointing at it in warning before I leave the bathroom to dress.

"Ah," Lady Devereaux trills as I find my way down-stairs fifteen minutes later. "About time, girl."

"Sorry," I mutter, scanning the sitting room in search of Casper or Kincaid, or pretty much anyone who would be an ally in this situation. A moment later Art enters from the dining room with a mouthful of blueberry muffin and plants himself in the armchair in the corner.

"Mind if I watch?"

Lady Deveraux doesn't reply so I assume she doesn't care. I suppose Artemis would have to be good enough, though I'd really been hoping for Kincaid or my tiny terrifying demon kitty.

"We'll train each morning at dawn," Lady Devereaux says, fixing her reflective stare on me. "If you aren't down here waiting for me, you will not train that day."

"But Kincaid said—"

"That I must train you," she snaps. "But I will do it on my terms. Is that clear?"

I swallow and nod, standing awkwardly in the center of the floor. What now?

Lady Devereaux rises on shaky legs, and I notice how she has a hunch in her back and how the skin on her forearms hangs off the bones as though there's nothing else there. No substance. She hobbles around me, muttering to herself, and I feel her poking and prodding at me on the inside and have to press my fingernails into my palms to keep myself from shoving her out.

I'm not even sure I could if I tried, though, so I don't bother.

"Asmodeus says you aren't aware of your parentage."

It's not a question, but I answer anyway. "No."

She huffs, coming to a stop in front of me. Hunched as she is, she's an entire head shorter than my five and a half feet.

"It's unnatural," she sneers, licking something black from her yellowed front teeth. "The light of your soul is the brightest I've ever seen in a Diablim. If I didn't know any better, I'd have said you were Nephilim straight off. But I can sense the darkness in you. You're Diablim all right."

She continues muttering to herself for a moment before seeming to decide something. "Asmodeus said he has a Spirit Scepter. That you used it to commune with Malphas. I've never heard of such a thing. The original seven don't have souls any more than a daeva does or the demon that stole a fair-sized chunk of yours."

"Can you get it back from him?"

She ignores my question and goes back to her chair, plopping into it like she weighs the same as someone twice her size. Dust wafts up from the old fabric, twinkling in the slanting afternoon light.

"I think I'd like to see you wield the Scepter."

"Not gonna lie," Artemis says, mouth full with another bite of muffin as he polishes it off. "I kind of want to see that, too."

"*Quiet*," Lady Devereaux barks and Art shuts his mouth and melds even more into the chair where he sits.

I wished he listened to me so easily.

"Run along and fetch it," she says. "Asmodeus likely keeps it in his quarters."

"Where is he?"

Her eyes bulge at me. "Do I look like his keeper? Go and fetch it so I can see what I'm working with here."

Artemis leaves the room when I do, and I get the sense he doesn't particularly like the idea of being alone with the old woman either.

"Where did Master Kincaid pick her up?" he asks as we ascend the stairs.

"Infernum."

His jaw slackens. "Is that where you were last night?"

I didn't tell him, not because I was hiding it, but because I really wasn't sure what Kincaid wanted Artemis to know or *not* know about what we were doing. He didn't seem overly happy the last time I blurted out our plans. But then again, he *did* let Artemis come with us through the Underbridge so…

"Yes."

"How was it there? They say it's the best of all the cities."

"Who says?"

"The Diablim at The Freakshow. They said it's like hell on Earth, which I guess for them is like saying heaven on earth, right? Must've been pretty cool, huh?"

I pinch the bridge of my nose, headache returning. "I don't really know," I admit. "I remember a weird church with a bunch of naked people and Belial sitting on a throne surrounded by headless statues of saints. After that everything's sort of a blur until we got to Devereaux's house. It was hot as hell, though. I do remember that."

His brows lower at my description. "You had some, didn't you? That's why you were all wrecked this morning. You tried Angel's Tears."

"Not on purpose."

He snorts. "Right it just *accidentally* found its way into your nostrils, then."

"I don't have to explain myself to you. Go take a nap or something, isn't that what children do?"

I know he won't be offended so I feel no remorse as I split off from him to go to Kincaid's bedroom. In fact, I'm sure he'd be more than happy to take the suggestion. The kid sleeps more hours than he's awake.

I rap at the door and wait for a response, but none comes and dread pools in my belly. For one, because I don't want to go into his room without his permission. For two, because I'm pretty sure if I don't bring that Scepter downstairs, Lady Devereaux is going to remove my soul from my body. And for three, because if Kincaid isn't in here, then where is he?

He said he wouldn't leave me alone.

Grounding myself with a long breath, I enter, flinching when the door lets out a shrill squeak. "Kincaid," I call into the dark, feeling around the wall for a light switch.

When I find none, I blink into the dim, letting my Diablim eyes adjust.

My lips part at what I find, and I open the door a little wider, letting some more of the light from the hall inside.

It's trashed.

I recall the terrible sounds the day we returned from Ford's house. The smashing and shattering and banging and shouting when Kincaid locked himself inside of his room for nearly three days.

His bed, once a masterpiece of whittled and expertly crafted mahogany beam and frame, is in splinters. The bench at the end is upturned, the legs broken. Several gaping holes in the wall the size of monstrous fists leak plaster down onto the floor like tears from empty eye sockets.

It's destroyed.

I know he's coming from the smell. That strange sulfuric odor permeates the air a moment before a burst of hot hickory and smoke takes its place.

Warm air tickles my ankles from behind, and I turn to find him behind me, a billow of quickly evaporating mist around his boots. His staff clutched in the blackened skin of his palm. He isn't fully in his demon form, but his arms are black to the crease of his elbows, and his horns remain out, as they have for some time now.

I find I'm getting used to seeing them there, feeling like there's something missing when they are not.

He sweeps the room, concern knotting between his brows. "Is everything all right?"

"I..."

"Are you hurt?"

"No, I—I was just..." What was I doing?

Kincaid watches me warily as he shrugs off his jacket and sets his staff down to lean against the wall by a crooked nightstand. There's something about him that's setting me on edge, and I don't think it's that his demon form still hasn't fully retracted. He looks…tired. Exhausted is more accurate.

His cheeks are sullen and his features are all pinched, wound tightly like coils of string around a top.

"Where did you go?"

"I had to speak to Belial," he replies, sitting heavily on the bed to remove his boots. He tosses them carelessly to the floor and scrubs a palm over his face.

"You said you wouldn't leave."

I can't help it, something about knowing he wasn't here—that he likely hadn't been for most of the night makes me more than a little uneasy. I'd been passed out, completely dead to the world for nearly twelve hours, and he wasn't here.

"I didn't have a choice, *Na'vazēm*. Belial would've come here if I hadn't and that wouldn't bode well for anyone in Elisium."

He sighs heavily and untucks his shirt, pulling it up from the back until it's over his head, leaving his chest bare. I try not to stare at the dip where his torso narrows into the belted waist of his jeans. The curve of his Adonis belt.

Vaguely, I recall Kincaid promising to speak to his brother later that night, but after our conversation with Lady Devereaux, everything is sort of blank for me. I scarcely remember getting into bed, never mind the trip home.

I had to have been unconscious.

"The mortals are growing uneasy," he says in a distant voice, gaze fixed on a crack in the wall opposite the bed as he thinks. "The general population isn't aware of our presence in the Fallen Cities, but their leaders are. They know that two of the seven are gone. Mortals who've ventured into Astrum and Delirium aren't returning in much more concerning numbers than before."

"That's their own fault." I can't help the haughty tone of my voice or the sneer from forming on my lips. "They were the ones stupid enough to enter."

I knew that despite all of my curiosity, when I still believed myself to be mortal, there wasn't even a lick of a chance that I'd have willingly entered one of the cities.

They were idiots.

"You aren't wrong, *Na'vazēm,* but that isn't the only concern."

I sit next to him on the bed and crane my neck to see his expression, finding hollows beneath his eyes that weren't there before. A weight settles like an anvil in my gut.

"A group of Diablim in Delirium have begun an assault on the barricades of the city. It will take time to wear them down, and the mortal attempt to make repairs just as quickly, but..."

He needn't say more.

So long as the Diablim continue, they will find a

way to break through. Our rocky truce with the humans will be at an end.

"I've dealt with it for now, but it's only a matter of time before the city devolves into chaos."

"What can we do?"

Kincaid shakes his head grimly. "Eliminate them."

I gasp. "The entire cities?"

There has to be another way.

"If we don't, the mortals will get what they wanted from the start."

"What?" I prod, wishing he would look at me. Wishing he would stop looking like a man burning alive from the inside out.

"A celestial war. They've always wanted the angels to clean up the dark *stains* on their land."

That didn't make sense, though. Why not just do it themselves? "Why don't they just nuke the cities? The mortals, I mean? The cities are contained. No mortals around them for miles in most directions. There would be minimal loss of life."

He tips his head to one side, a question in the set of his brow. "Because then we would reopen the gates of Hell and unleash an age of darkness on the Earth."

He must see the shock in my face because he smiles devilishly, and I grip the rumpled blankets under me to regain control of my features. I'm not afraid of him.

"You can do that?"

He considers me for a moment.

"No one of us can, but the seven lords together could."

I wonder why they haven't, but don't ask, not sure I want the contents of Hell to empty. There are enough devils here already. "But now there are only five," I mutter.

Kincaid's fingers brush over my knuckles as he settles his hand atop mine. "They don't know it would take all seven. For now, all they need to fear is that at least one of us will survive to make good on the threat."

"And the angels? Why haven't they initiated a war?"

I don't say the other thing I'm thinking. That if there are the same number of angels as there are demons and most of the latter are in Hell, then Kincaid and his cohort are likely *vastly* outnumbered. Especially considering it seems Angels may travel between the mortal plane and their own at will. Whereas the remains of the demon race are trapped in a nightmare sealed behind unbreakable gates.

It hardly seems fair.

Kincaid doesn't answer right away, just releases my hand. "I need to shower."

Remembering why I am here in the first place, I jump to my feet and smooth down the starchy creases in my shirt. "I need the Scepter. Lady Devereaux wants to see me wield it. To test the limit of my power, I think. She doesn't believe that I spoke to Malphas."

His brows draw together. "Then a shower will have to wait."

"It's in the closet over there." He points to where a door hangs slightly crooked in a slender doorframe. Inside, I can see the edge of the gray blanket that covers the Spirit Scepter, wrapped in silvery rope.

When I turn back, Kincaid is naked. He strides to where a clean pair of half-folded jeans lie on the floor and pull them on over his bare legs. I catch a smirk before I am able to peel my eyes away, clearing my throat as I rush to grab the Scepter from the closet. I touch it quickly at first, testing to make sure it isn't going to just suddenly activate and raise whatever dead things may be lying dormant beneath the floorboards of his mansion.

"It won't bite."

I turn to find Kincaid watching me, his lips twitching as he holds back laughter.

"*Paige*," he calls, but I've already stormed out of the room.

Bastard.

I bet he wouldn't be cracking jokes if *he* were the one who had to touch the fucking demon stick.

15

Lady Devereaux dozes in the armchair where I left her.

Her head tipped back against the backrest, mouth gaping and expression soft and drooping.

She doesn't look so mean that way.

"What!" She jumps awake, sleep-slowed gaze swimming through the room until her eyes narrow on me.

I take it back. She couldn't ever possibly not look mean.

"Someone needs to teach you some manners, girl. When I ask you to go and fetch something, I expect that you'll—"

"Lady Devereaux. Have a nice nap?"

She fumes at Kincaid as he strolls into the sitting area and goes to lean against the wall next to the entry to the library. He looks at her with a challenge in his stare, and I know he's purposely trying to taunt her.

I'm not sure if I want to chastise him for poking fun at an ornery old woman or applaud.

I'm leaning toward the latter.

If this morning was any indication, my training with Lady Devereaux was going to be anything but enjoyable.

Something in the way she looks at me tells me she would relish breaking me. She would examine all the pieces with a keen eye and then leave me half put back together, satisfied to know what makes me tick and uncaring of what I'd need to go through for her to figure it out.

"Asmodeus," she says by way of greeting. "I didn't realize you'd returned."

"I told you I wanted to be present should Paige use the Scepter. Is your mind affected by memory loss these days?"

She shakes her finger at him and bares her teeth. She goes to say something I'm sure will be equally biting, but Kincaid silences her with a raised hand.

"And it's *Kincaid* here in the city. No one calls me Asmodeus."

"A pity if you ask me. *Kincaid* is a ridiculous moniker for a demon."

Kincaid crosses his arms and gestures to where I stand, holding the Scepter at arm's length. "Do you think it best if we go outside?"

"I'm perfectly happy right where I am. Go on, girl, unwrap it."

I look to Kincaid for affirmation, but it's Lady Devereux who speaks again.

"Is she always so difficult?"

Kincaid's brows rise. "You have no idea. I'm sure the pair of you will be a match made in Hell."

That's reassuring.

I wet my dry lips and set to untying the knot in the silvery rope with fumbling fingers when I hear Artemis coming down the stairwell outside the room.

"Here, let me," he offers, and I gratefully pass him the Scepter, my stomach flipping.

It barely takes him three seconds to get the knot loose, and the rope falls away, slinking to the floor with a *hiss* against the thick fabric.

"Pass it along," Lady Devereaux rushes him, and Artemis lets the heavy blanket drop from the Spirit Scepter.

Immediately, the whispers rush in, the beads around my wrist rendered useless. The pressure on my chest is bone-crushing, but I know that once I take hold of the staff, it'll ease.

"Is that…" Devereaux's question trails off. "Bless my black heart. It can't be. Only two were ever forged. How did it end up here?"

"I'm not sure," comes Kincaid's reply, but my eyes are sealed shut against the barrage of whispers and the crushing weight on my chest.

"Likely he brought it himself during the opening of

the gates. Have you told him it's here on the mortal plane?"

"No."

I tune them out, not understanding what the hell they're talking about anyway. As terrifying as it was the last time, the promise of the rush of power is enough to make me want to rid myself of eight hundred pounds of spirit pressure on my lungs.

Kincaid slips over to us so quick I barely notice him as he slides the bracelets from my wrists just a second before I reach out and snatch the Scepter from Artemis.

The rush is just as I remember it, except this time it doesn't feel like my heart stops dead in my chest. I'm prepared. *Ready.* The same wind that swept out over the graveyard before sweeps into the room now, and I twitch at the sound of broken glass as the windows bow and break from the force of it.

Lady Devereaux and her chair have fallen back. Her socked feet flounder in the air and her arms flail.

Kincaid and Artemis are in the entry now, pressed against the farthest wall. Where Kincaid watches with a sort of reverence in his eyes. Pride for his purchase. Artemis looks like he might be sick, and it makes me want the wind to stop.

As I think it, they are able to lift their heads from the wall and take a step forward. It dawns on me that I am the ruler of the Scepter and not the other way around.

I try to rein in the hurricane gusts, pulling them back to myself. It works, but only to a point. It's too hard to concentrate with all the whispering, shouting, spitting voices in my head. Nothing like the assault at the cemetery, though.

Here, there are fewer spirits to contend with, and I feel them out, filing through them as if they were pages, searching for one of two familiar voices.

Kincaid and Artemis each take one of Lady Devereaux's arms and help her to stand. She leans back from me with an arm raised to shield herself from the still bustling wind. Her eyes go wide at what she sees, and I find myself smiling.

She's afraid of me.

Why should I enjoy that?

I shouldn't. Yet, I do.

"Incredible," she says and I have to read her lips to make out the word.

"She is," Kincaid says next to the old Necromancer, his voice deep enough to penetrate the wind and cacophony of voices filling my ears like cotton and lead.

"Paige!" Kincaid shouts over the roar. "Can you hear them?"

I shake my head. "I'll keep trying."

I shut my eyes, drawing on the raw energy rushing through the staff and into my veins. Inhaling to slow the deafening thunder of my pulse, I begin to sift through the voices again, searching for the ones I want.

"Call them to you!" Lady Devereaux croaks as she sinks back into the now-righted armchair, leaning over the edge of it.

I shut my eyes once more and speak their names in my mind.

Dantalion.

Malphas.

When nothing happens and I hear no new voices, I repeat their names over and over, beseeching them to come to where I can hear them.

I feel them before I hear anything different. Like a dark stain on an otherwise blank canvas. As my eyes fly open, they come into view. They are a mirage on a dark horizon. Distant wavering images—like they are merely silhouettes of themselves. With white eyes and dark chasms for mouths.

I keep calling, drawing them in. Closer. An ache forms on the precipice of my skull, and I wince, gripping the staff harder.

"Impossible." Lady Devereaux's voice finds me in my focused dark, and I turn to see her staring out into the distance, too. Past the doorway to the library and beyond, into the chasm opened up by sheer force of my will. To where the two shadows wait in the fathomless deep. She can see them, too.

"You can't draw them both," she calls to me, hustling to her feet and rolling up the sleeves of her dark gray blouse. "Focus only on one of them, send the other back."

I do as she says, shoving back the shadow to the right in favor of the one on the left. The one pushed away vanishes, evaporating into nothingness, as the other becomes clearer.

His features come into focus. Hair like a halo of gold on his head and eyes glittering like fresh cut sapphires in a face so sharp it could also have been cut from stone. Dantalion.

His mouth moves, but I cannot hear him. The din of incessant chatter in my mind is too loud. "I can't hear him," I grit out as a droplet of blood finds its way into my mouth. "The voices—they're too loud."

"Draw him closer," she instructs. "Pull him in as you would a tug rope. It won't be without some effort."

No shit.

I envision the rope. Try to mentally reel it in.

"Good. Now you must shut out the others. Shore up your mental defenses. They are tools for you to wield and command and nothing more. You must push them out."

I try, but it's too much. I can't pull in Dantalion and shove out the other voices at once. Not even with the help of the Scepter.

"I…can't."

"You can."

I have to stop doing one thing to succeed at the other. I hold fast to Dantalion but do not draw him any farther, screaming internally with all the force I have for the other spirits to get out.

It works, but not nearly as well as it did in the graveyard at Bellefontaine. There, I'd barely had to think to wield the staff and silence the voices. The level of available spirit energy there was much greater, though.

Once I have them all at bay, I resume pulling Dantalion's spirit to me, sighing when his moving lips begin to emit sounds I can hear.

Dantalion looks at me incredulously, his face a mask of horror. "How?" he asks, and his voice is a shaky whisper carried to me on the breeze. It almost sounds like it's coming through a radio.

"Beats me," I manage through the internal strain.

"Are they here?" Kincaid bellows, searching the air where both Lady Deveraux's and my eyes are fixed.

"Dantalion," I reply. "He's here, but I don't know how long I can hold on to him."

The dark abyss from where he came hovers at his back. Its pull on him like a super magnet.

Kincaid straightens. "Dan, what happened? Who did this to you?"

Dantalion's dark blue gaze falls to his brother and a flicker of vivid agony crosses his features. It hurts to look at him.

"I don't know."

I reiterate the message to Kincaid while Lady Devereaux looks on in stunned silence and Artemis just kind of watches from the corner of the room.

"It…it was like being torn apart. But from the inside," Dantalion explains. "Then…nothing."

There's almost no trace of his holier-than-thou attitude anymore. He isn't the same demon who twirled me around the gleaming dancefloor at the Midnight Court. But I supposed dying would do that to a person.

"Spirit magic," Lady Devereaux muses when I finish telling Kincaid what he said. "Must be."

Kincaid's face hardens. "Do you have any enemies, Brother? Diablim or demons in Astrum who would want you dead?"

"Many." Dantalion scoffs with a dark laugh. "But none capable of this."

Kincaid grits his teeth as he considers this, his fists clenching and turning black as he works through the puzzle before him.

"What was done with my body?" Dantalion asks, and I pose the question to a now mostly-demon Kincaid.

He cocks his head. "It's entombed at Hightower."

Dantalion's lips press together and I get a sense of what he's truly asking, a sick feeling roiling in my belly. "You want me to try to put it back," I guess.

His eyes glimmer with hope when he levels them on me again. "Can you? Is it possible?"

I look to Lady Devereaux for guidance, and her wrinkled face pinches. "*This* shouldn't be possible," she sneers with a frustrated wave of her arm.

It's as much of an answer as we'll get.

"Would your body not be, you know, decomposing?" I ask, shuddering at the thought of putting life back into a worm-eaten corpse. That wouldn't be living. It would be something else. Something terrible.

DANTALION GIVES A SLOW SHAKE OF HIS HEAD. "IT'S A celestial vessel. It does not decay."

"Is that true?" I ask Kincaid, who just stares confusedly until I remember he can't hear his brother. "That his body doesn't decay?"

Kincaid's brows lower in thought, and then he nods. "It's true."

A sharp pull at my core tells me we're running out of time, and I rush to redouble my efforts to hold Dantalion steady in this plane. To keep him from vanishing into the other. "I'm losing him!"

Kincaid steps forward as he would reach out and hold his brother here in this world, but then his hands return to balls at his sides, and he drops his head. "I'll find who did this to you, Brother," he promises. "You will be avenged."

The rope snaps, and Dantalion is shot back into the dark like a star slung across an empty galaxy.

16

The Spirit Scepter is released and with it every remaining ounce of my energy and the barriers I erected in my mind vanishes.

Kincaid catches me before I can do too much damage to my knees as I fall. He tugs on my bracelets and brushes his black hand up and down my back until my breathing evens.

"Artemis," Kincaid growls. "The Scepter."

The cloth slides over it and Artemis rushes to wrap it up with the silvery rope, lifting the phantom weight from my chest enough that I can breathe properly. I blink through the blur in my vision until I can see Lady Devereaux standing opposite us.

She stares into the library, into where the void had been, her hands in fists on her hips.

"What does this mean?" Kincaid asks her. "Can she bring him back? Can she bring them both back?"

I cough and blood splatters over the back of my hand, coating my tongue in the earthy, metallic taste.

As though drawn by the scent, Lady Devereaux whirls. "How should I know?" she snaps at Kincaid, looking between him and me with clear distaste.

"*That place,*" she hisses, pointing at nothing. "The one you called him from; it's not an earthly plane. It was something else. I've never seen anything like it. So how should I know its rules? Hmm?"

Kincaid breathes heavily against my back, and I find myself just wanting to melt into him. To close my eyes and let the rhythm of his breaths take me into sleep.

"*Devereaux,*" Kincaid warns at her tone, but she only scoffs at his threat, flicking her knobby fingers in the air as though he were a fly to be swatted.

Artemis kneels at my side after discarding the Scepter out in the hall. "Can I get you anything?" he whispers.

When I don't answer, he adds, "That was *badass.*"

Kincaid glares at him, and he backs off, scuttling out into the hall, muttering something about getting me a drink.

"This level of power is dangerous," Devereaux tells Kincaid, and I wonder if she'll insist on her earlier suggestion of killing me.

She doesn't.

Kincaid bundles me up into his arms, lifting me as though I weigh no more than a sack of flour. I let my head fall into the crook of his neck and let my eyelids flutter closed, daydreaming of my bed. "I brought you here to teach her how to control it. Are you saying you can't?"

"No. But there are limits to what I can teach her."

"Then teach her everything you can!"

"This power..." Devereaux trails off. "It isn't just dangerous for those around her. It could tear her apart, Asmodeus. A half-mortal body isn't made to withstand it."

There's a long silence before either speaks again, and I stir from the edge of sleep to the rumble of Kincaid's rich baritone.

"Are you telling me I have to choose? That if I push her to do this, she could die?"

Lady Devereaux doesn't answer, and I push myself to stay awake, to see her face. But moving is really and truly out of the question now. I manage to open my eyes though, and look up at the haunted demon clutching me to his chest.

"I'll do it," I murmur, drawing his yellow-eyed gaze. "Whatever it takes."

He looks like he might argue, but stops himself, the muscles in his jaw flexing.

"I'll be careful." The words are barely a whisper as the cloying embrace of sleep gets its claws under my skin. "I'll be fine."

Kincaid lifts his gaze again to Lady Devereaux, and I can see a thick vein pulsing in his neck. His demon-form is receding, leaving a sickly pale color in its wake.

"If anything happens to her, I'm holding you personally responsible."

My weight shifts in his arms as we leave, and I let my eyes fall closed again as we ascend the stairs and take a sharp left. A moment later, cool silk is against my cheek as Kincaid lays me in his bed. His scent envelops me, and I sigh.

Casper's meow brings me back to the surface for a moment, and I watch as he enters Kincaid's bedroom, lifting his rear as he stretches out from a nap. As though nothing at all is amiss. As though I didn't open a rift in the space time continuum or whatever the hell I did.

"Protect her," Kincaid orders the sleepy kitty, removing his hands from my back to draw a blanket up to my chin.

Casper chirrups in reply, as though he were a mother cat calling her kittens and hops onto the bed, nuzzling into the top of my head as though he were a crown of fur.

"I have a traitor that needs dealing with." Kincaid seethes. "I'll be back as soon as I can."

I shudder, and if it were possible, I'd feel sorry for the Diablim who kidnapped Artemis. But it's not, so I don't. Choosing to smile instead as sleep claims me.

17

It's night when he returns.

I sense him before I see him, stuck somewhere halfway between asleep and awake. Like a disturbance of air or the presence of something in water, making its volume greater. It's his soul, I realize as I peel back my eyelids, squinting into the shadows.

He leaves his bedroom door slightly ajar after entering, a sliver of diluted moonlight the only light illuminating the space.

"Kincaid?" I venture, knowing it's him in my bones, but needing to reassure my mind. All I can see of him is a silhouetted outline as my Diablim eyes take a moment to adjust.

"Yes, *Na'vazēm,*" he replies, and I don't like how he sounds.

I push myself up, and Casper jolts awake and hisses

before darting for the door. There's a sound like rustling fabric and his jacket falls to the floor. I stand, not liking his silence.

There's too much unsaid in it. It's strained. Tepid.

I find him as my eyes adjust, running a hand down his arm until a tacky smear just below his elbow catches my fingers. I know the smell, so I don't have to look, but I do anyway.

His hands are coated in half-dried blood and smears of it mar his arms all the way to the crooks of his elbows. There are spatters over his tunic, too. And when he lifts his head, I can see that there's an arc of more vibrant red just below his jaw.

Blood didn't spurt like that on its own. A chill passes over me, raising the hairs on my neck.

"Zak?" I ask.

"I've made an example out of him."

Dead, then. *Good.*

Unperturbed by the blood, I take his tacky hand in mine and wordlessly lead him through the carnage of his bedroom toward the bathroom.

He can't go to bed like this. He'll ruin the sheets. I'm not sure why that matters, but right now, it's one thing I can control. One thing I can actually help with. So, I do.

I flick on only one of the two light switches in the bathroom, illuminating only the small scones on the wall next to the mirror above the double-sinked vanity. It's enough to see by but not assaulting to the eye. I consider the tub, but with the sheer amount of crimson covering Kincaid, it's just not a good idea. Not unless he wants to soak in bloody water.

It takes me a couple of minutes to get the water running just right in the giant glass-encased shower. There are too many buttons and levers, but eventually I get it to a temperature just below scalding and have the water gushing from the large oval showerhead hanging above as well as the regular showerhead set high up on the midnight blue tiles.

The breath whooshes from my lungs as I'm swept inside, passing through a stream of hot water until my back connects with the tile wall. Kincaid pins me there, breathing heavily as he glares into my eyes.

Water rushes over his black hair and down his neck, washing away the blood from his collarbone, soaking through his clothes and mine.

"*Why?*" he demands, breaths sawing out between bared teeth.

"Why what?"

My blood sings with adrenaline and my chest meets his with every heavy inhale. Wet hair falls into my eyes and the hot water soaks me all the way through every layer of my clothes now.

"Why are you doing this?"

I don't know what he means. "I-I'm not doing anything," I argue.

"You are doing *everything*."

His grip on my wrists tightens, pressing them harder into the steam-warmed tile.

I don't break eye contact as he brings his face closer to mine. For a heart-wrenching second, I think he's going to kiss me, and I'm afraid I might spontaneously combust if he does, but he stops just shy of it, his breath whispering over my wet lips, softer now.

"Why would you willingly risk yourself…"

He isn't asking me. I'm not sure he wants to know the answer. But I'll give it to him anyway.

"You aren't what I thought you were."

Kincaid looks doubtful at my response, his eyes narrow. "Not the monster you imagined?" he asks, and his voice drips with disdain.

I shake my head, remembering my own glee at seeing Ford dead on that metal slab at the morgue. Remembering how it felt to rip the souls from the bodies of the Old Crones at The Freakshow.

…my lack of caring at the fact that my demon is covered head to toe in someone else's blood. That even now, it stains the bed of the shower a muddy pink.

"Not any more of a monster than I am."

"*You're wrong,*" he says, but I don't think I am.

I don't think I've ever been more *right.*

I shake my head again, scattering droplets of water over his chest. I'm not sure what I was about to say but it's lost to the press of his mouth on mine. Hot and insistent, he kisses me with a passion bordering on insanity.

My arms come free from his hold, but before I can lower them, he's tugging on the hem of my shirt. It peels off my skin, and he lets it fall to the floor with a wet *slop*.

The rest of our clothes swiftly follow, and he presses himself to me, the silky slide of our bodies against one another driving me mad. I gasp and tremble, the chaotic onslaught of sensation and emotion unwinding me from the inside out.

His hands slide to my waist, and he presses himself into my hips, his hard length brushing against my belly. I tip my head back in a moan, but he swallows it up with another kiss. My head spins, and I'm surprised I remember how to breathe as my hand moves low between our slick bodies, wanting to feel his erection.

As my fingertips brush over his tip, he groans. And as I wrap them around his girth, he shudders, thrusting into my palm. Our lips come apart, and he stares down into my eyes, breathing heavily. The unspoken question passes between us, and I nod fervently.

"I want you," I manage, my voice no more than a broken utterance of words. I sound unsure, but the truth is, I've never been more sure of anything in my entire miserable life.

Kincaid's golden gaze never falters, keeping scrutinous watch on me as he runs his fingers down my torso, eliciting shivers in their wake even though I'm so hot I feel like I might melt down the drain.

When he reaches my throbbing sex, he exhales

lustily, finding it already slick with its own silky wetness. When he pushes two fingers inside deliciously slow, I think I might die of wanting him. My hips move against his fingers, trying to urge him to go deeper, faster, but he splays a hand over my belly, pinning me there as he teases little sounds from my body.

His smirk tells me he knows exactly what he's doing to me, and I think two can play at this game. I redouble my efforts on his cock, pumping my hand up and down on his shaft. I have no idea if I'm doing it right, but judging by how his jaw tightens and his eyes close in ecstasy, I have to assume I'm doing it right.

If he keeps doing what he's doing, I'm going to shatter; I can already feel it coming, making my legs clench and my toes curl.

"Kincaid." I moan, and he withdraws, bringing me back from the edge. I cry out at the loss, but he's already shifting, nudging my legs apart with one of his thighs as he dips down, strong arms lifting me, guiding my legs around his waist.

His erection sits level with my folds, and I grip him tight, nervous but so *so* ready. He only hesitates for a moment before pressing my back hard into the wall and guiding his cock inside. It's slow at first, and I can feel *everything* as his thick girth stretches me, pushing in and *in* and *in* until he's seated inside me to his hilt and I let loose a shuddering breath against his throat, fingers digging into the solid muscle of his back.

It hurts. *Burns*. But I don't want him to stop.

The next thrust isn't nearly as gentle as he rears out and slams back in with a grunt, filling me in a way that makes me ache. The pleasure-pain sensation is splintering something inside me, and the next time he thrusts I cry out, leaning in to bite down on his neck to keep from screaming. That only seems to turn him on more. He pumps into me harder and faster, driving my pelvis into the wall with each thrust.

His hands curl around my thighs, holding me open for him as he drives into me wildly, savagely.

I tip my head back in a whimpering pant; my breaths come faster now than even the staccato rhythm of my heart racing in my chest. Kincaid presses his lips to mine, his teeth dragging over my lower lip until I taste the tang of blood and he sweeps in, his tongue drawing another splintering moan from deep within.

He slows his thrusts as he kisses me, pausing to grind his hilt against my slick mound, teasing the bud until I feel a quickening sensation awaken in my core. A flood of warmth pools in my womb and I have to pull back from my demon's lips, needing the oxygen to stop my head from spinning.

"That's it, *Na'vazēm,*" he whispers against my cheek, "Come for me."

He increases the pace, propelling me higher, winding me tighter for the release. I'm going to fall.

"*Now,*" he roars, and I feel his muscles tighten. His release sends me over the edge, and I plummet.

He devours the sound of my release with his mouth,

moving against me as my climax thunders through me, sending sparks of color flashing against my eyelids until I sag in his arms, utterly spent. I listen to the drumbeat sound of his heart as he holds me to him, sensing his soul reach out to mine from some dark place deep within.

18

Something wakes me in the night. It can't have been very long since we fell into bed because my pillow is still damp from my hair, and I can still feel the memory of Kincaid inside me so clearly I have to wonder if he might still be.

The ache between my legs and low in my belly makes me squirm anew, reaching out sleepy hands to find him in the bed. But they come up empty, and I hear the rustle of denim over skin, and I force my eyes to open.

"What are you doing?" I mumble, blinking the sleep from my eyes. "Come back to bed."

I'm hungry for him still, I realize. Even with the mild aching pain inside, I want to do it again. *Now.* When Kincaid doesn't answer me, I prop myself up on an elbow and force my body to wake.

"I can't, *Na'vazēm.*"

When he bends to pull on his boots as well, my desire ices over with something far more potent and much less pleasing. "Where are you going?"

He comes to kneel by the bedside and draws my hands to his lips, brushing them over my bony knuckles. "It's Lucifer. He calls me home."

"What? Lucifer? As in the devil?"

"He *is* my commander," Kincaid replies, and though he tries for a light tone, maybe even for sarcasm, it falls flat. Sounds strained. "I won't be long. He's demanded my return to Hell. I assume for an audience about Malphas and Dantalion. It was only a matter of time before he found out."

I'm wide awake, and the blankets fall from my body as I sit up, swinging my legs off the bed.

"When will you be back."

He shakes his head.

"Can't you just say no? Stay here?"

He frowns. "No, *Na'vazēm.* I cannot."

I get up and begin searching the floor for my clothes before remembering it's all still sopping wet in the bottom of the shower. "Well then I'm coming with you. I just need to go get some cloth—"

"*No,*" he growls, the guttural sound enough to make me pause before I can exit the room. "As far as I'm aware, Lucifer does not know of your existence. I'd keep it that way."

He comes to me, pulls me to him. I shudder against the cool denim, not yet warmed by his flesh, but let him embrace me. "Why don't you want him to know?"

"I'm not sure what he'd do," Kincaid admits, whispering the words against the top of my head. "You shouldn't be able to travel between realms. He'll want to know why. He's been searching for a way out of the pit since his last escape."

"He'll think I'm somehow his way out?" I venture a guess, not liking how that sounds.

He nods against my temple. "Something like that. I'm not prepared to take any chances. You'll stay here. And I will return as swiftly as I'm able."

I wrap my arms around his middle and squeeze tight before letting him go. "Train," he orders me. "Train as hard as you can as *carefully* as you can, and *do not* leave this house. I'm going to leave word with my guards to set up a watch perimeter outside."

I open my mouth to speak but have no idea what to say. I hate the insinuation that I'll have time to train while he's gone, which means he won't be back in twenty minutes, or even an hour. Or even a day.

My chest caves in on itself as he walks out the door, leaving me feeling oddly small. Like he's taken a piece of me with him.

I DON'T SLEEP THE REST OF THE NIGHT. I PACE AND worry for hours before deciding that is an entirely useless waste of my time and go to find clothes and drag a comb through my hair. I'm already in the sitting room, satiated from a half-decent breakfast of apple and stale bagel, when Lady Devereaux hobbles down the stairs.

She lifts her gaze to me as she enters and with a pursed lip nod, she says, "Good. Let's begin."

We start with the basics, and Artemis comes down to join us some time just before noon.

Lady Devereaux allows me to use her Diablim soul as a training dummy of sorts, but only allows me to go so far. We don't use the Scepter because she wants to get a better gauge of my abilities without its magnification.

She doesn't admit it, but when it only takes me two tries to gently lift the edges of her soul from her body, I can tell she's impressed.

We work on energy exchange for a time after that, having no other living things to practice on that we wouldn't mind killing by accident. Artemis suggests using a rat or a mouse and Lady Devereaux sends him down to the basement to find some.

Truly, I think she did it to get rid of him and stop his incessant asking of a million questions, but I don't say that. I hope he doesn't find any mice, even though I know many live in the walls of the mansion. They tried to steal my food just after Kincaid purchased me and brought me here. And I hear them scratching in the walls at all hours of the night.

I don't want to kill one, though. They're too cute. They didn't do anything wrong.

Now, if Artemis could somehow procure a serial killer from the basement, I'd be happy to use *that* soul as practice.

"Pay attention," Lady Devereaux tuts, snapping her fingers in front of my face.

I groan.

"You need to draw the energy of the spirits, but keep their influence at bay. You keep letting them in up here," she knocks on my skull, and I flinch, batting her hand away, "when you need to let their energy flow through *here*." She jabs me in the chest, and I rub the spot, glaring at her.

"I just need a minute," I say through bared teeth. My focus started waning sometime around the sixth hour, and now at the ninth, my brain feels like mush.

I need lunch, but judging by the slant of light outside the broken window where one of Kincaid's henchmen stands guard, it's closer to supper.

"You won't get *a minute* out there," she argues. "So I won't give you one *in here*."

I roll my eyes, earning myself a spiritual slap. She pulls back on my soul as though it were an elastic band and lets it *snap* back into place. It's disorienting and burns as it settles back into the chasm of my physical body. I hate it.

And she knows it.

"If you try to draw energy from spirits but don't

block them, you'll be possessed every day to Sunday. And if you don't *try,* I'll let them ride you into the dirt without batting an eye."

My shoulders sag, a thousand scathing retorts and curse words I've never before uttered threatening to be forcibly evicted from my mouth.

"Try drawing from me instead," she adds, going back to her armchair. "Try to draw my energy."

I move to get nearer so that I can touch her, remembering how I needed the contact to be able to draw energy from Artemis the last time, but she lifts a finger to stop me. "Ah-Ah," she trills. "That's cheating. Contact makes it easy. You'll draw my energy from right where you are."

I inhale deeply to maintain calm and close my eyes, letting out my feelers until I can sense her soul, but that's not what I'm to draw on, I could end up detaching it. I only want her energy. I try to differentiate between the two, to pull only energy instead of her actual soul, but it doesn't work, and she hisses as I pull on the wrong thing.

Artemis wanders back into the room empty handed, and she sighs in exasperation.

"Pour me another drink, boy," she calls to Artemis. "I think we'll be here a while yet."

Artemis casts me an apologetic look before vanishing through the library to raid Kincaid's liquor stash for Lady Devereaux for the third time today.

While he's gone, I sink onto the carpet and let my

body fall back until I'm leaning on my elbows, wishing I could keep going. Take a nap right here on the musty carpet.

I glance to where Artemis is two rooms over, digging through bottles to find more of the Port wine the Necromancer likes.

"There's something I wanted to ask," I blurt before I can change my mind.

Her eyes narrow on me. "Well, go on, girl. Out with it."

"The lords, you said it was spirit magic that was killing them. I was there when Dantalion died. I saw his soul leave his body."

"Is there a question somewhere in there?"

"If it's spirit magic that is separating their souls from their bodies, is there any way I could…stop it? Do something to counteract whatever magic is killing them?"

She cocks her head at me and a swath of her silvery hair falls forward, brushing against the wrinkled skin on her chest. "You mean to try to save him, is that it?"

My gaze falls, and I swallow past the lump in my throat, mouth suddenly cotton dry.

Is it stupid to think I could? I don't know.

What I do know is it would be even stupider if I didn't do everything I could to try.

"Do you think I could?"

"I can't answer that until I know what's causing—"

"There must be a way," I insist. "Something you could teach me that could help if…"

I can't finish the sentence. I don't want to imagine having to watch Kincaid die in front of me and be powerless to stop it.

Lady Devereaux nods slowly, her stare going blank as she thinks. "All right," she says finally. "We can focus some of our effort on offensive tactics, and how to reanimate a corpse with the soul of the deceased. If you're to even *attempt* to reimplant the soul of Dantalion, then you'll need to begin learning how to now. It took me years to do it just right."

"We don't have years," I say in a breath, a flutter of panic taking wing in my chest.

"I didn't have a teacher," she says with a slow-spreading grin and a wink. "And you happen to have the best one on this good green earth."

19

We go on like that for days.

They all start to meld together. If it weren't for my counting the hours since Kincaid left, I wouldn't even know that it'd been precisely four and a half days now. Hedging on four.

Training keeps me busy, but not busy enough to forget that someone out there is stripping souls from the bodies of ancient demon lords. That Kincaid could already be a soulless corpse somewhere before I even had the chance to do a damned thing about it.

I convince myself it isn't true, that I would feel it somehow if anything happened to him, but I know that's probably not true.

"Quit sulking," Lady Devereaux chastises at dinner. Artemis has become quite the little cook this week, having found a few dusty cookbooks in the cupboard above the fridge. I think he's happy to have something to keep him busy aside from watching the training sessions.

I also think he really likes demanding all manner of different ingredients from Kincaid's henchmen outside, casually mentioning that their lord wouldn't be pleased if they didn't get what he asked.

We've had mostly burnt lasagna, a horribly overcooked turkey, and a runny quiche, but the meals were all better than our usual cold canned goods and crackers. Tonight, though, he's really outdone himself, and I wish I had the stomach to enjoy it because the spaghetti and meatballs are likely the best I've ever tasted, and it was one of Ford's usual meals.

"Is it that bad?" Artemis asks, and I look up to find him watching me. I stop pushing the bits of beef and noodles around on my plate and lay my fork down.

"No, Art, it's actually really good. I'm just…not that hungry, I guess."

"You're *always* hungry," he argues, and he isn't wrong, except for right now.

Tori's words replay in my mind. They've been my mantra since he left. *He always comes back.*

He always *comes back.*

All I can do is wait.

I sequester myself in the basement after dinner, needing the cool solitude of thick cement and stone walls. My mind is too tired to bother trying to ward off the spirits that now stay clustered around the property at all hours of the day and night. The bracelets help, but it's still tiresome trying to ignore them.

There must be some otherworldly gossip mill churning out there. Either that or they're simply drawn to my power. Perhaps it's both. I make a mental note to ask Devereaux about it tomorrow and yawn, stretching out my neck and shoulders in the recliner and jostling Casper in the process.

"See," I tell him, pointing a finger to the screen. "That's who I named you after. Isn't he cute?"

Casper makes a noncommittal sound and drops his head once more, nuzzling his little pink nose into his paws on my knee. "Come on," I tell him through another yawn, scooching him off my lap since he likes to hiss at me when I lift him up. "We should go to bed."

It's easy to lose time down here where there isn't a single window to let in natural light. For all I know it could already be the wee hours of the morning, and I'll have to get up after only a few hours of rest. My Diablim blood makes that more easily possible, but Lady Devereaux's all-day-long lessons would wear out even a full-blooded demon, I think.

Casper pauses on the stairs, his body going rigid while only his tail twitches in the air.

"Casper?"

His hackles rise, and he launches himself out of the basement, making my heart leap into my throat. A flood of power reserves leak into my veins and I feel the rush of spirit energy chase away the ice biting at the tips of my fingers.

I rush to chase him, praying that Artemis is safely tucked into his bed with the door locked. Praying that it's only a rat or that one of the henchmen has come too close to the house.

But then I sense him. His soul a speck of growing dark in a bright sky.

"Kincaid!" I call, rushing through the kitchen, the dining room, the library and through to the sitting room.

A strange scent permeates the air and for a heart-stopping second I think it's not him after all. That it's someone else. Someone *very* unwelcome.

But then I see him. He kneels in the entryway, steam rising from his shoulders. His face and clothing coated in a fine grayish dust. He lays down a long stone coffin on the marble tile to the staccato sound of hastening footsteps upstairs.

My shouts obviously woke the others.

"Kincaid?" I venture, coming to kneel down in front of him on the other side of the strange coffin hewn of ivory stone.

He looks up and it takes a minute for his eyes to focus on me—for him to see me. His brows unfurl and his lips part as recognition dawns.

"Na'vazēm."

"What happened?"

"About time you returned," Lady Devereaux tuts

from the base of the stairs, clinging a fluffy emerald robe around her frail bones.

Kincaid shakes his head and brushes a hand over the coffin, his fingers tremble slightly, and I grip his hand, forcing him to look at me.

"What happened?" I urge again, looking between him and the stone box. "Is this…is this Dantalion?"

His lips tighten. "Someone tried to take his body."

Devereaux and I share a look. I wonder if she's thinking what I am. That they didn't mean to *take* it. They meant to *destroy* it.

"They fled when I arrived at HighTower. If I went after them, I would've risked someone finishing the job."

"HighTower? Who was it? Did you see?"

Kincaid slides his hand out of mine and pushes up from his knees to stand, watching the coffin with a wary eye. "No. But only us three and the soul of my brother knew I interned it there."

His ochre eyes lift to mine, and in them I see barely restrained rage. "You've been to HighTower before," he adds in a deadpan monotone. "It's my fortress."

In Hell.

That was where he transported us from the Midnight Court.

His gaze slides to Artemis and Lady Devereaux, and a sneer curls his lips back from clenched teeth.

"Kincaid," I gasp, stepping over the coffin to block him. "They didn't have anything to do with this."

Artemis goes whiter than the sheet he has clenched around his middle, and Lady Devereaux folds her arms over her chest, clearly not at all impressed by his insinuation. She obviously doesn't know him well enough to know that the look on his face right now spells only one word: *murder.*

When he doesn't back down, I try another tactic. "Wouldn't that be where anyone would expect you to keep it?"

He falters, some of the tension leaving his jaw.

"I mean, where else would you keep it? And how do you know whoever it was didn't look in a hundred other places first before finding it at HighTower? Besides, they were here with me the whole time."

He holds up a hand to stop me, and I shut up, dropping my hands from his overheated chest.

He pulls in a shaky breath and rolls his shoulders.

"It's someone from Hell, then?" I muse, trying to make sense of it myself.

"Or someone who can travel there," he says in a growl, and I hate how he isn't looking at me. He can't possibly think that I…

No.

That's ridiculous.

"Okay," I say, beginning to pace the small space between Kincaid and the others. "So, one of your other brothers then? They're the only ones who can, right?"

He shakes his head. "It can't be them. I've had tails on all of them since Malphas."

There may be a lot of love between Kincaid and his brothers, but I was starting to understand that love didn't mean there was also trust. I suppose a millennium of life could really create a layered and very chaotic relationship.

"Besides, none of them wield spirit magic."

"With an accomplice, then?" Devereaux rasps, clearing her throat.

Kincaid pinches the bridge of his nose for a moment before lifting Dantalion in his stone box from the floor with ease, hefting the long slender piece onto his shoulder before striding from the room.

"I think maybe I'll just go back to bed," Artemis mutters, and I give him a little nod before he goes.

Lady Devereaux follows me as I follow Kincaid through to the dining room where he has laid Dantalion's coffin atop the dining room table, scuffing the surface irreparably by the look of it.

He shakily pours a glass of amber liquid, though he does not drain it, just takes a few small swallows as he watches the coffin as though it will grow jaws and spill all of the secrets he wishes to know.

"Powerful spirit workers are extremely rare," he says, his gaze never leaving his brother. "I can think of only three even *possibly* powerful enough to accomplish this, and two of them are here already."

Is it weird that I should feel pride at his offhanded compliment when there's a corpse between us?

"With an amplifier, perhaps," Devereaux offers.

"Something like the Spirit Scepter could bestow enough additional power on the wielder to—"

"There *is* nothing like the Scepter."

"Except for its twin, of course," she argues. "They were forged in Hell for Lucifer himself half a millennium ago. I haven't the faintest idea how one could have wound up here, but if one has, then you can be sure it's possible the other one is on this earth as well."

I lick my dry lips and sit carefully at the head of the table, near the head of Dantalion's corpse. "You said you knew of three who were powerful enough. That leaves one who could be responsible. Maybe they have the other Scepter?"

"It's still doubtful. His power doesn't compare to yours, and I'm not even certain you would be strong enough to pull a demon's soul from his body."

I don't disagree with him even though I think he might be wrong. I've only just begun my training. I don't say so, but I have no doubt that with enough years of practice, I would be able to do just that.

I'm not sure how he would feel to know that.

Devereaux lifts her chin. "With enough vigorous training and a great many years, anything is possible, especially with a tool as robust as one of the twinned Scepters."

"Do you know where I might find him?"

Devereaux snorts, and I get the sense she knows exactly who he's referring to. Did all Necromancers know each other, then?

"Well, normally, I'd say drowned in liquor at one of the pubs in Aetherium, but, if he truly is to blame for this, then I don't know."

Kincaid dumps the rest of his drink down his throat and sets the heavy glass down on the liquor cabinet. "I cannot keep leaving. It isn't safe," he grunts.

I go to his side and refill his glass for him, taking a small sip before pressing it into his hand. "If you don't, then it's only a matter of time until one of your other brothers fall."

The pain in his gaze tells me it was both the right thing—and the wrong thing—to say. What I've left unsaid hovers there, too; it could be him that's next.

"You have to do this."

...because I can't lose you.

I've never *had* anything or anyone to lose before. It's a terrifying thing—caring for another living being. I'm not sure I like it.

Devereaux wanders over and digs out Kincaid's Port, unstoppering the bottle by yanking the cork out with her yellowed teeth.

"She's right, you know."

She takes a long pull and swipes at her mouth with the back of her hand. "If you lose any more lords, it'll all fall to shit. We'll all be sent straight back to the pit we came from. And I don't know about you, but I'd rather not commingle with all the souls I sent back there over the last four-hundred years."

She takes the bottle with her as she goes and we

hear the stairs creak and groan under her weight a couple moments later.

"Will you go then?" I ask when Kincaid makes no move to leave or speak.

"Tomorrow," he decides. "I'll have Tori stay here with you until I return. And I'll double the guards on the property. You'll be safe."

"It isn't me I'm worried about."

Without warning, he sets down his glass and hauls me to him, burying his face in my hair. Small bits of rock and plaster dust fall onto my nose and cheeks, but I don't care.

"Just eleven more days. I need your help, *Na'vazēm.* Just a little longer and I'll see you home. You'll be safer there."

I move to pull away, confused at his meaning, but he just holds me tighter, his grip near crushing as he shakily sighs against my temple. I'm going to ask him what he means when he pulls away, but all rational thought abandons my mind as he presses his mouth to mine in a tender kiss that sends shivers skating down my spine and makes my toes curl.

"To bed?" he whispers against my lips, and it's my turn to shut him up, kissing him again, harder this time, making his chest rise sharply with a lustful intake of breath.

He passes me the remnants of his drink and then scoops me up into his arms, almost making me spill its contents all over the both of us. He spares a glance for his brother before carrying me from the room.

"Will he be safe here? Shouldn't we bring him with us?"

A muscle in his jaw jumps, and I smooth it back to resting with the brush of my palm. He presses into my touch, grip tightening on the back of my knees. "As safe as he can be," he purrs. "And soulless or not, I'll not have my brother's corpse bear witness to the things I intend to do to you."

20

"Did someone say there was a party at this address?" Tori asks when I open the door to her grinning face the next day.

"There will be no such thing," Kincaid warns, appearing at the top of the stairs. His voice alone is enough to trigger a visceral response in my body, and I press my legs together, clearing my throat and dropping my gaze as I wave Tori inside.

She sets down two grocery bags with a cheeky smirk and shrugs. "Party for two will have to do, I suppose," she relents.

"Hi," I say, breathing in her lavender when she wraps her slender arms around me.

"Hey, kitten, how you holding up?"

"Fine." I try for nonchalance, but I can tell right away she isn't buying it. "You know you don't have to bring groceries every time you come, right?"

"If I didn't, who would make sure there's food in this house?"

"Artemis has gotten surprisingly good at ordering Kincaid's henchmen around. We have more than can fit in the fridge at this point."

"I'm making steak and roasted sweet potato wedges tonight," Artemis says with a prideful grin, rushing past Kincaid to bound down the steps. "You eat meat, right?"

Tori tugs him in for a sideways hug and fluffs up his hair, messing it up even more than it'd already been.

He detangles himself from her with an indignant chuckle, blushing like the boy I sometimes forget he is.

"Yes, I eat meat," she laughs. "I like mine rare, though. Don't fuck it up."

"Yes, ma'am." He salutes her and leaves while Kincaid makes his way down and Tori gathers up her bags from the floor again.

"It's not *just* groceries by the way," she says, holding out one of the plastic bags to me. I peer inside, seeing clear jars of something pink and purple and a roll of black material with little silver things poking out one end. "I noticed your hair was getting a little…"

I wince. "Is it that bad?"

She bites her lip and shuffles the bag to inspect my ends. "We'll get it all fixed up."

"Do you even *know* how to cut hair, Tori?" Kincaid asks, taking the bag from Tori's hands to inspect it himself. He unrolls the thick cloth to reveal a few pairs of sharp silver scissors and clips and combs.

She snatches it back from him. "I'll have you know I've been cutting my own hair for years and I'm pretty damned good at it, thank you very much."

A small grin tugs at one corner of his mouth, but it doesn't reach his eyes. He places a large hand on Tori's shoulder and the aloofness drains from her expression. "Don't let her out of your sight."

Her ashen skin flexes around her temples and the conviction in her voice would convince any man of the veracity of her words. "I won't. I promise."

Their staredown lasts another couple of seconds before Kincaid squeezes her shoulder and then goes to retrieve his staff.

"Come on," Tori prods me, looping her arm through mine. "Let's go do something about that hair."

"But..." I trail off, wanting to say goodbye. But before I can untangle myself from her, Kincaid's staff taps twice on the tile and by the time I turn around, he's gone.

"So is there a method to this madness?"

Tori gestures vaguely at my head, lifting a few strands of hair to get a better look at the sections beneath.

"Um," I say, trying to relax. "More pink toward the top and purple at the ends."

It all just kind of looks like a mess of pale grayish-pink at the moment and I don't blame her for wondering.

"Cut?"

"Whatever," I shrug. "It grows fast."

She grins, and I think I should maybe take that back. Tori pulls off her short black pixie cut like a fucking supermodel. I doubt I'd get away with looking half as good in the same haircut. "Maybe…not too short though?"

She pouts. "Fine. Just a trim then."

"You don't have to do this, you know."

I take the drink she passes me. It's a cocktail of some kind that she's been mixing on top of my dresser. A dark pinkish liquor mixed with a vibrant blue one and topped up with something fizzy and white in a label-less bottle.

It smells like candy but with the bite of alcohol beneath all the sweet layers. "Trust me, you'll like it."

She twists the caps off the colored dyes and stretches gloves over her hands. "*But* your body might not tomorrow. Just drink lots of water before bed, yeah?"

"Thanks." I take a sip, and the sweet artificial raspberry flavor slides down my throat with ease. "*Mmmm.*"

"Told you."

She sections off my hair, and I'm reminded of the first time I asked to have my hair done at a real salon. It was my fifteenth birthday, and I had it done bright green. I bought four more colors at the salon before I left, knowing that Ford wouldn't deny me on that one special day of the year, and especially not with an audience about.

No, he'd stand there with a strained smile, arms crossed over his chest as he leaned on the wall and watched from a near distance, refusing the hairdresser's offer for him to sit in the waiting room.

From what I remember, Tori definitely seems to know what she's doing.

"And by the way, I'm not here just because Kincaid asked me to be here. And I'm not doing this because I feel any sort of, I don't know, obligation or pity or whatever. You're good shit, Paige, and you *really* needed your hair done. Kincaid just gave me a good excuse to close up shop for a bit."

My face flushes, and I'm not entirely sure why, maybe it's the drink.

"Sales have been shit anyway," she continues. "Besides, I'm always there when a friend needs me."

A friend? Is that what we were?

I'd never had one before.

Well, aside from Artemis, but that was different. He was like...a surrogate little brother or something. I felt a sense of responsibility for him.

"I've never really had one," I admit before I can think better of it. "A friend, I mean. You'll tell me if I do it wrong, right?"

She pulls her glass from her lips and nearly spits out her drink as a fit of laughter takes her, but the laughter quickly fades when she sees the look on my face. Maybe realizing just how serious I was about that first part.

"I'll tell you," she offers and goes back to separating and lifting out strands of my hair. "Now, let's get this looking good enough to make Kincaid want to see it in a just-fucked style, yeah?"

"Tori!"

"You cannot honestly tell me you didn't rip up your V-card and set it on fire for that bastard."

She raises a brow and I…I don't know what to say other than, "What's a V-card?"

Tori looks at me like I might be from another planet.

"Your *vir-gin-ity,"* she enunciates, and I flush scarlet, taking a long, slow drink of my cocktail to soothe the flare-up.

"I *knew* it." Her violet eyes sparkle, and she grabs a chunk of pink dye to get started on my roots. "Tell me everything. Is he hung? Does he like weird shit? I bet he likes weird shit."

I'm not going to lie, it makes me so much more at ease to know that she *doesn't* know what he likes. Because if I had to compete with the angelic goddess that is Tori…

Well, I just couldn't.

"*Um*, define weird shit."

"Shit, girl. We're going to need another drink."

She finishes hers and moves to snatch mine away,

forcing me to down what remains in the glass so she can refill it. A giddiness spreads through my nerve-endings, and I find I'm grinning like an idiot and can't stop.

"Maybe a little less of the 'ol nectar of the gods for you, huh?" she says, taking notice of my expression with a slightly pained smile. She puts less of the fizzy clear liquid in the next one for me, running to the bathroom to top it up with a bit of water instead.

"Do I want to know what I just drank?" I ask, giggling when she sets the next drink in my lap.

She sucks her lips in and thinks about it for a second. "Probably not. Maybe don't tell Kincaid, either, 'kay? I kind of forgot that you're, you know..."

"New?"

"Yeah, that."

"Aren't you going to have another one?" I ask, gesturing at her empty cup.

"Nah. One of us needs to stay vigilant against all the terrors of Elisium." She leans in, lowering her voice to a whisper. "But if you ask me, I think the only thing you're in danger of is dying of boredom. I'd lose my mind locked up inside day and night."

I chuckle and take another drink as she settles back into doing my hair. "So this *'weird shit.'* "

She glances up at me in our reflections in the vanity mirror with a quirk of her perfectly manicured brow.

"You want a run down?"

"I'm not entirely sure what's *normal,* so..."

"Okay. We'll take it from the top then. Hmm, where to start."

She taps a finger against her chin, leaving a smear of vivid pink there that I'm not sure she notices. "Ah! I know. Butt stuff. That's always a good place to start."

I NOW HAVE A WORKING KNOWLEDGE OF EVERY FORM OF sexual *weird shit* on the planet. And maybe some stuff that she picked up from those who came straight from H-e-l-l because...*why*? Just why?

It turned out what Kincaid and I had done thus far was fairly typical, and I had to wonder if he was taking it easy on me. If he was holding back. Surely after a lifespan as long as his you would acquire some...*different* tastes.

Like acquiring a taste for scotch. Or finding after years of thinking you hated olives that somewhere down the line you must have changed because they don't taste so bad anymore.

Regardless, I had to hand it to Tori. Unlike last time where she seemed to worry just as much as I did, she was really keeping it in check this go-round. Maybe it was because she sensed just how stressed I was about the fact that Kincaid left, and even more so now that it'd been nearly two days. She was acting as my one-woman distraction. She took over after daily training with Lady Devereaux was through until I would inevitably fall asleep.

I knew it might take some time to find the other necromancer, but I wished he would just check in. Was it that hard to use that staff of his? Did it drain him each time like using the Scepter drained me?

"Come on, let's go tan on the roof or something," Tori says, coming out from my bathroom after a shower. I'd given her my room and taken to sleeping in Kincaid's. Taking it upon myself to clean up the mass of destruction he seemed to be perfectly fine living in on the rare nights he was home nowadays. I could do nothing about the holes in the walls, but c'est la vie.

It was as good as it was going to get.

"Tan?"

"Yeah," she replies, tipping her head upside down to scrub dry her short, black hair. "You know, like, under the sun. It's hot as hell today and there's still a couple hours until sunset."

"I know what tanning is, I just…"

"Would rather mope about instead?"

I sigh dramatically. "Fine. I don't have a bathing suit though."

"No need."

She drops her towel.

"No one will be able to see us on the roof. We'll go nude. I hate tan lines anyway."

I supposed modesty wasn't a trait Nephilim *or* Diablim possessed. I tried not to stare before I spun around.

"Or you could lend me a bra and panties if—"

Downstairs, the blaring noise of a bell chiming echoes up to us, halting Tori mid-sentence. I didn't think I'd ever heard that doorbell before. The short burst of adrenaline in my blood kickstarts my ability, and my mental feelers extend out almost of their own accord.

I sense them. They aren't demons. Not even Diablim.

"It's…"

"*Uh,* Tori," Artemis calls from outside in the hall. "There's a really intimidating angel dude at the door. He brought friends."

"Fuck," Tori hisses and rushes to pull back on her towel, clearly flustered. It sets my nerves even more on edge.

"Angels?" I question her. "Why would they be here?"

She flits her violet eyes to mine for a brief second, and in them I see a worry that turns Artemis' chili sour in my belly.

"Stay up here. I'll deal with it."

She quickly tugs on yesterday's shirt and hops into her pants as she leaves the room, foregoing undergarments completely. I move to follow her out the door, but she grips the door frame, her eyes bursting with the glow of igniting power within. "Don't," she says. "I don't know what they want. It's safer if you stay in the house."

But they're angels, I want to argue, *doesn't that mean they're the good guys?*

I nod instead, remembering the way the diviner looked at me that day at the police station in St. Louis. With disgust. Hatred. And the way the red-headed angel at the Midnight Court looked on with smug satisfaction while Dantalion fell. While Kincaid left and Tori dragged me away.

No, I think. *Perhaps they aren't the good guys after all.*

I hear the door creak open downstairs, and I tiptoe down the hall. I won't go down, I just want to be able to hear better. At least, that's what I tell myself as I move to join Artemis at the edge of the bannister, pressing myself tightly against the wall to avoid notice. Casper joins us, rubbing himself across my shins in a weaving pattern as though nothing is the matter. Useless demon cat.

"What are they doing here?" Artemis mouths, sidling up next to me.

I shrug. "Don't know."

"*Tristane,*" I hear Tori say, her voice a disinterested drawl. "To what do we owe the magnanimous pleasure of your company. Ah! Isolde. You're here, too. How nice."

"Victoria," the angel replies. I know it must be him because his voice sends shivers up my arms. Its honeyed, malice tone making me want to swoon and run for the hills all at the same time. "Is the master of the house at home?"

"Afraid not. Though I'm guessing you already knew that."

I swear I can *hear* the angel smiling when he speaks again. "Too bad. We've come for a brief audience with his newest *acquisition.*"

"Then you'll have to come back when her *master* arrives."

"I have orders, Tori, don't test me."

"As do I, *Tristane.*"

My pulse thrums against the barred cage of my ribs, and I must look as worried as I feel because Artemis' hand curls around mine, holding it tight. "Don't worry," he whispers. "She'll get rid of them."

Why wasn't I so sure?

And where the *hell* were Kincaid's henchmen. He said he'd be doubling the number of them outside guarding the house.

"What's this?" Devereaux's croaking voice joins the others downstairs, and I'm not sure why, the woman is the bane of my existence, but I feel almost compelled to rush down there and shoo her away.

She's old. She's Diablim. She shouldn't even be here.

"Devereaux," Tristane croons. "I'd ask how you managed to get here, but I think I may already know."

I hear her huff in reply, and without looking, I already know she'll have her hands on her hips. She'll be staring him down like he's a stubborn toddler and she's going to have to get out the wooden spoon. It's a look she's given me a hundred times this week.

"We're here to speak with Paige. She'll need to

accompany us for a brief conversation, and we'll deposit her back here unharmed when we're finished."

"Unlikely," Devereaux mutters. "Like Victoria already told you, pinhead, the master isn't at home. You'll have to come back."

"Are you disobeying a celestial order?" Another voice, feminine with bite, rises above all the others. "Because that would be *very* unfortunate for you."

"*Wait,*" Artemis hisses, but I've already slipped my hand out of his and am halfway down the stairs.

"We can talk here, can't we?" I ask, gripping the bannister so hard I hear the wood groan under the pressure of my fingertips.

Tristane stares past Tori to find me. He's just as I remember him, but with the sun staining the sky a bright and vivid gold behind him, he looks even more like an angel now than he had before. His aura pulses with almost blinding light, making his polished copper hair look more gold. His steely eyes burrow into me while his lips slither into a full smile, showing two straight rows of teeth.

The woman at his side has a strong aura, too, but it's clear to see she is not a full-blooded angel. Even though her perfect blonde hair would be the envy of any god.

"*Ah,*" Tristane expels cheerfully. "There you are."

Tori cuts me a scathing glare before turning back to face the angel and his retinue of three Nephilim. "I'm afraid Paige won't be joining you. Come back when Kincaid returns."

I peer out, looking for help from the outside and catch sight of two of Kincaid's men standing sentry at the bottom of the drive. I suppose messing with angels isn't in the job description. Useless.

Tori moves to close the door on them but Tristane's polished mahogany boot stops her from closing it completely. Long fingers grip the edge of the door and force it open. The smile is gone from his angelic face when he regards Tori this time, and I rush forward to wrap my hand around her wrist and tug her back.

Judging by the stark white of her fisted knuckles, she was thinking about *punching a fucking angel.*

I'm no rocket scientist but that has *bad idea* written all over it.

"I don't want to hurt you, Victoria," he warns her, and in his icy stare, I see a flicker of truth. He really doesn't want to hurt her. I look between them and for the first time notice a tension there. Something more than just the fact that he's come to collect me and she's here to keep me safe.

"It's fine," I blurt. "I'll go with you."

"The fuck you will," Tori snarls, peeling my hand from her wrist.

I grab her hand and jerk my chin back toward the stairs. "Can I talk to you for a second?"

Her nostrils flare.

"Can you give us just a minute?" I ask the angel on

our doorstep, and he removes his hand from the door but doesn't budge from blocking our ability to close it.

"A minute. No more."

I drag Tori toward the kitchen, and Casper pads along cheerfully behind us, his little bell jingling.

"You can't trust them!" she growls once we're more than likely out of earshot.

I shake my head. "I don't, but I'm not going to watch them hurt any of you just because I refuse."

"Kincaid will *kill* me."

"Let her speak to them," Devereaux chimes in, hobbling into the kitchen with us. She gestures to Casper who's resumed brushing himself over my shins and purring like an idling engine. "If they meant Paige any harm, her bonded demon would be protecting her."

"Her…*what?*"

I grimace. "Guess I forgot to mention that."

"No shit."

"It won't do us any good to start a war on Asmodeus' doorstep while he's away," Devereaux adds.

"He'll kill all of us if they hurt her," Tori warns the old Necromancer, and she purses her lips.

"I'm afraid we'll die much sooner if we refuse their order. I'm still quite strong for an old lady. So are you and so is Paige. But I doubt even the three of us can stand up against a full-blooded angel and three high level Nephilim."

Tori groans loudly and grabs a fistful of her hair as

though she means to pull it out. I get the sense that Devereaux is right, and she doesn't like it one bit.

"Fine," she says finally. "But you are *not* leaving. If they want to talk to you, they can do it here."

Devereaux and I share a look.

We both know that if they demand it, I'm not going to be able to argue.

"How hard would it be to strip an angel of his soul?" I ask, just wanting to understand if I have any chance at all should it come to that.

She smirks. "Just as impossible as stripping a demon's."

I wink, trying to lighten the mood. "So not *technically* impossible, then."

"I can't believe this shit," Tori mutters to herself before brushing past me back the way we came.

Devereaux and I follow, and Artemis gathers up the courage to come downstairs to join us, though he hovers just behind.

Tori jabs a finger at Tristane, and I might be imagining it, but her skin turns even more ashen than usual. It looks...almost like stone. "You can talk to her right *here*, asshole. You have five minutes."

Tristane shakes his head, sending his loose copper hair sweeping over his brow. "I'm afraid that won't do. We'll be taking Paige to a secure location. But you have my word we'll return her before dawn."

"Dawn?" Tori demands. "What the fuck do you think

this is? Rent-a-Necro? You don't get to just come here and take her."

All traces of humor leaves Tristane's expression, replaced with the threat of violence. "You're lucky my orders are not to keep her, Victoria, or else I'd happily *take her* from you and *not* return her at all."

Tori splutters for a response, her face turning a shade of ashen red before the color fades and her shoulders slump, defeated. "Then take me, too. I've been charged to watch over her, Tris. You know what he'll do to me if he returns to find her gone."

"Your safety is not my concern anymore. It was your choice to deal with demons. Now you'll reap the consequences of that decision."

"Tell him I made you let me go," I offer to Tori and then turn to Art and Devereaux. "If Kincaid gets back before I do, tell him I'll see him at dawn."

"Let's not make a fuss," Devereaux replies, patting me lightly on the bum to send me staggering forward. "Just take care of our girl. If she's harmed, you'll have more than one pissed off demon to contend with, you hear?"

Tristane nods his understanding and takes me by the arm, sending a *zap* of spirit energy coursing through me like a fucking live wire. He recoils as though burned and moves to press a hand to my lower back instead, prodding me down the stairs to the open door of a black town car.

"You made the right choice," Tristane tells me.

I whirl on him when we reach the car, letting the full force of my power show in my eyes. I can already feel the edges of his soul. I wonder if he can feel the press of my phantom fingers trailing over its ridge. "Don't make me regret it."

21

They take me across the city. Farther than The Freakshow, more to the west, to the outer edge of the city's limits. By the time the car stops outside of an old, decrepit church, the sun is just moments from poking its bright brassy head down below the horizon.

I raise a brow at the weathered facade of the building. It's hardly what I imagined when they said they were taking me to a 'secure location.' I mean the doors are wide open. One of the stained-glass windows to the right of it is broken, and the jagged remnants are like razor sharp teeth in a dark maw.

Something about this doesn't feel right, and I'm uneasy when the woman named Isolde gets out of the backseat before me and holds the door open for my exit without a word.

"Here?" I ask, doubtful. Trying to hide the fear

clawing up my throat.

One...

Feel it.

Two...

Breathe.

Three.

Lock it up.

"Yes," Tristane replies, shutting the door to the passenger seat after stepping out to join Isolde. "Here."

All righty then. Here we go.

I follow them inside, avoiding the shattered glass on the overgrown pathway leading up to the door. I hadn't had time to grab my shoes. Didn't really think about it at all when we left.

A jacket might've been nice, too. The blistering heat of the day left with the sun, and my skin bristles with the lick of cool wind rushing through the open doors and broken windows.

"Down here," Tristane beckons, and I fall into step behind him, the other three Nephilim drawing up the rear. Boxing me in.

I scan the interior for exits and find one across the building, near a rubble coated stage, just behind a tall wooden stand with a microphone perched on its edge. I store the information away and keep going, letting Tristane lead me down a narrow hall and then down a wide staircase.

It seems to get cleaner as we go. There is no rubble on the steps. No signs of decay in the corridor of the floor beneath the pew-strewn room upstairs. When we go down another flight of stairs, the cold gets to be so much that my teeth begin to chatter.

And, like I knew it would but prayed it wouldn't, my sixth sense dulls. The spirit chatter always at a low hum in my mind all but vanishes. The spark in my blood splutters out.

The walls are too thick. We're too deep underground.

At the bottom there is a bank of heavy metal doors in neat rows to either side. In front, there's a pair of double doors. The kind with heavy silver locks and wire-mesh in the windows.

Tristane holds one of those open, revealing a bright space within. Steeling myself, I step inside.

There isn't much here. Just a clean, stainless-steel table and two chairs. One on either side. The walls are a crisp white, making the off-white of the drop-ceiling look horribly dirty by comparison. There isn't a speck of dust anywhere. Not a whisper of the decrepit building sitting two floors up.

If I hadn't walked through it myself, I wouldn't even believe it was the same place. And yet it is. I contemplate whether there has always existed an otherworldly prison beneath the floorboards of this old church, meant for the Diablim who escaped Hell one of the first two times, or whether it was a new addition: built only when there were enough Diablim to claim the city for their own.

Not that it matters.

"What is this place?"

Tristane smirks, and I don't miss how the others remain outside as the white door swings closed behind him. "Some kind of interrogation room?"

It reminds me of one. At least, from what I've seen in films and read in books.

"Very astute observation," he says and falls gracefully into the chair farthest away. "Please. Sit. The faster we get through these questions, the faster I can have you returned."

"And if I give answers you don't like?"

His gray eyes narrow, giving me all the answer I need.

They don't intend me harm…so long as I cooperate. So long as I am not a threat, and right now, they don't perceive me to be. I just have to keep them thinking that.

I fold myself into the chair opposite him and wrap my arms around myself to stave off the chill, wondering how the hell I'm sweating when I'm at a point near freezing.

"So, it's *Paige,* right?"

He already knows that, so I don't bother replying.

"All right. Paige, let's begin with the basics. My orders are to find out your history. Where you came from. Why you're here. *What you are.*"

"Then you'll be disappointed," I say, rolling my shoulders back and dropping my hands to my lap. Not wanting to appear weak. "Until a few weeks ago, I didn't even know I was Diablim. I still don't know what I am other than that I wield spirit magic."

"So we've heard. You caused quite the stir at The Freakshow but that isn't what has my superiors curious about you. What has them curious is how a Diablim new to the city, with supposedly no prior knowledge of her heritage was able to travel to Hell and back…and *live*."

The way he's watching me makes me want to squirm, and I have to suppress the urge with laced fingers and a clenched jaw.

"I don't know."

"I'm not buying that."

"I'm not selling it," I snap before I can stop myself. "It's the truth. I *don't know*. If I did, I would tell you."

I'm not sure if that last part is a lie, but I throw it in there for good measure, trying to subdue him.

Tristane leans forward, resting his elbows on the table. His pale blue button-down is rolled up to the creases of his elbows, and where his biceps lie hidden beneath, the fabric strains. With his fingers steepled at his lips, he considers me.

I'm not naive enough to think he believes me, but how far will he go to get the truth? If he meant me harm, Casper would have done something. Devereaux said it herself.

So, I have to believe he isn't going to torture me to get answers.

...but he will keep me here until dawn.

I could almost laugh at how *not* scary that is. To think that a month ago I was chained to a chair and zapped with high voltage electricity over and over again for hours and now *this* was all I had to contend with?

It really put things into perspective.

So when he stands, nearly knocking his chair back, his face a twisted mask of fury, I don't even flinch. He couldn't possibly do anything to me that would be worse than the things I'd already endured.

How had I forgotten that? How had I forgotten my strength?

I snorted to myself. "So, if that's all," I drawl. "I guess you can just take me back to the house. I could even put in a good word for you with Asmodeus, make sure he doesn't hunt you down and kill you for forcing me to go with you."

"*You little—*" He cuts himself short verbally and physically. Half launched over the table I thought he might actually strike me, but he won't, and it brings a smirk to my lips that only infuriates him further.

He tosses the chair back and it clatters against the wall as he strides past, shoving his way through the door.

"Get me a diviner," he roars and there's a flurry of hushed responses before a loud blow silences all.

"*Do it.*"

Two sets of footsteps leave, padding in sync up the stairs.

"What should we do with her?" I hear the Nephilim called Isolde ask and strain to listen to Tristane's response.

"Don't let her leave this room. She can sit there until the diviner arrives."

"And if we can't get one here that quickly?"

"Then you better pray Asmodeus doesn't get back anytime soon because she isn't leaving here until I get answers for Elijah."

Heavy footsteps depart, and I assume he's left Isolde to keep watch over me. To make sure I don't leave. I like my odds against just one Nephilim, but I won't try to escape. Not just yet.

The diviner who gleaned that I was Diablim in St. Louis was of a lower-level, and I pulled away from him too quickly for him to get any more useful information from my mind.

But whoever Tristane hires to root around in my skull might actually be able to find something useful. Information I maybe don't want falling into the hands of angels, but it could be more than we already know.

Maybe the answer Kincaid and I had been looking for would be dropped right into my lap. Maybe I was finally going to learn exactly where I came from, and what I am, at last.

I settle in for the wait, peeling my bracelets off and stuffing them in my pockets...just in case.

22

Hours pass.

I start counting the seconds and minutes after Tristane leaves to pass the time, but I lose track somewhere around hour three when other thoughts begin to invade my mind.

It's amazing how easily they do that when I don't have the incessant chatter of the dead to drone them out.

I try not to worry about Tori, Artemis, and Devereaux, and what might happen to them if Kincaid returns to find I'm gone. It would be a lie to say that he wouldn't be furious. That he wouldn't blame them.

Closing my eyes, I send a silent plea to whatever god or devil will hear it. *Please let me get back before he's home.*

My legs are stiff from sitting in the same position, and I stretch them out, arching my back until my spine pops. A shudder runs up through the chair, vibrating in the seat, and I wonder if it's me who was shuddering, but then it comes again, and I press my bare feet flat against the cold floor, feeling a tremor below.

I lean forward in my seat, vivid images of zombified corpses playing like a movie reel in my head.

No.

It's not possible.

I can barely send out my mental feelers, my power is so suppressed down here. I can't have risen anything from the dead like this.

A distinct *knock* hits just beneath my hand from the other side of the floor, and I jump up, a short gasp flying from my lips.

Another reverberating *bang* beneath my feet and the floor splits. It heaves and then dips, caving in, and taking me with it.

The air is stolen from my lungs as I fall, bits of jagged flooring and busted concrete scratching against my arms and cheeks. I mean to scream, to call for help, but no sound comes out of my gaping mouth. It's like a sea witch stole my voice and no matter how hard I try I can't make a sound.

I hit bottom and clammy fingers clasp onto my ankle, dragging me down deeper into the dark away from the light.

Above, there's a barrage of sounds and then a brilliant white light as Isolde drops into the chasm with me, landing on her feet with a sword drawn.

A fucking *sword.*

I spin to find the face of the creature trying to drag me away and go colder than a corpse.

It isn't a reanimated corpse at all. It's a man. Or maybe it was once. I can't sense its soul, but I am certain without having to be told that it's a demon.

A sneer curls its pale thin lips and its large searching eyes glimmer in the light of the Nephilim's flaming sword. A forked tongue slips out of its lips, as though it can taste Isolde in the air.

"Let her go," Isolde demands, charging forward.

It's then I realize where we are, why it smells of rot and feces. It's a sewer, or at least, we are near to one. And judging by the gouged divots in the dirt and stone walls around us, this creature *tunneled* into the basement of the church.

I jerk my ankle, trying to find purchase in the hard-packed ground with my fingernails to heave myself away from the creature.

"I said let her go!" Isolde repeats, lifting her sword to swing.

But she's thrown back, her body flung as though no more than a doll, until she crashes against the wall of the upward climbing tunnel. She chokes and starts, her sword falling from her hands so that she can grip the metal bar protruding from her middle instead.

Blood streams down the length of it, coating her fingers, dripping from her wrists. I watch in muted horror as what I can see of her soul's light flickers and goes out.

The scream that'd been lodged in my throat echoes back to me now, the raw sound of it urging me into action.

I thrash and kick, landing a hard blow to the creature's face. It lets out a feral cry before trapping me once more, snapping something hard and sharp around my ankle.

I flip onto my back, ready to unleash whatever dregs of my energy remain on him. Ready to throw everything I have into ripping this bastard's soul from his bones regardless of the earth trying to block my energy.

But I don't get to do any of that. The instant I'm face up, bulging eyes lock on mine and a shadow passes between us before something hard knocks into my skull and my eyes flutter shut.

23

The smell of rot permeates the air. Almost stronger than the acrid taste of blood lingering in my mouth. It's hard to open my eyes. I can barely wiggle my fingers.

When I try to turn my body to get a look at what's making the strange scratching sound above my head, something hard bites into my wrist, forcing me awake. I jerk, trying to get it off, but it's latched on too tightly. I crane my neck to one side on the hard surface where I'm lying to find I can't move it because it's shackled in place with a pockmarked piece of iron.

My other hand won't move, either. My legs are fastened just as tightly. I lift from my knees, trying to bend the binds, to break them. But I can't. I try to draw on my power, sending out my mental feelers, but I'm met with cold resistance. I can't do it.

Blinking rapidly to clear my eyes, I try to get a sense

of my surroundings, finding hard stone walls on all sides that I can see. No windows. No *air*. The lack of it makes my pulse erratic. Makes it feel like there's an elephant on my chest. No doubt I'm somewhere deep beneath the earth, where my ability can't draw on what it needs to function.

"Come on," I grit out, tugging forcefully on the metal binds on my wrists—so hard that a line of fresh blood drips down onto the wooden table.

"It's no use, girl."

The voice is hoarse. The S sounds lengthen into hisses, slithering into my ears like worms.

I jerk and twist, bucking my back and lifting onto the top of my head to see the speaker behind me.

In a view upside down, he stands hunched at a narrow wooden workbench. The scraping sound I heard was him mashing something in a mortar with a pestle. His long bony fingers grind and twirl.

"Those are celestial bonds. And only *I* have the key."

"Who are you?"

Behind him, I see all manner of hammered metal objects. Hooks and blades. Flasks and a bone saw. And...I'm afraid I already know.

The Carver peers up at me from his work, showing two eyes that bulge from their sockets, one slightly askew. His thin, crooked nose seems almost to hang from his small, sharp-angled face. Little tufts of hair cling to a mostly bald scalp covered over in age spots and what looks like actual *rot*.

"My name is of little consequence and would only be defiled by your mortal tongue."

"You're the Carver, aren't you?"

There's a twinkle in his eye when he cocks his head at me. "So then you knew I would come for you? Why then, did you make it so simple?"

I breathe in deeply to try to quell the flutter in my chest, reminding myself that I am Paige St. Clare, and that whatever this fucker does to me, I can handle it. I've handled worse than him, haven't I?

It's that question that eats at me, because while Ford was evil down to his core, he wasn't what the Carver is. He wasn't a demon on Earth.

"Kincaid will find me," I warn him, but my voice thickens with something dangerously close to tears because I'm not sure he will. I'm not even sure where I am. But I *have* to be inside of Elisium. This creature, the Carver, he can't leave. He's trapped here just like all the others.

"He'll kill you," I threaten.

"Will he now?"

The glimmer is gone from Carver's eyes, he stares at me with unconcealed malice, slowly setting down his mortar atop the table before removing the pestle and scooping up whatever is inside with two of his fingers.

I've gotten to him. He must know that if he is found, he will die. If he's even a little bit worried I'm right, then I have to believe it's possible. That Kincaid *will* find me.

In the meantime, though, I need to find my own way out. There's a door near Carver's workbench. It's metal and has a keypad not unlike the ones on the doors at Ford's house. I won't be able to get out without the code. *Shit.*

I'll have to pay attention to—

"What are you do—"

The demon wrenches my jaw open and stuffs his fingers down my throat, making me gag. My entire body convulses as the taste of something sickeningly sweet mixes with the bile in my throat, and I'm forced to choke it down while he seals a dirty hand over my mouth to keep me from spitting whatever it is out.

His hand comes free a moment later, and I splutter, my stomach roiling at whatever it's just been forced to ingest. "There," Carver says. "Much as I'd love to see you squirm on my table, that just won't do."

My body twitches as it goes limp. My limbs are heavy as though filled with lead instead of muscle. *It's a sedative,* my mind supplies, and yet I am awake. I am painfully, *fully* awake. I just…can't move.

My neck feels disconnected from my head, and I can't be sure, but I think my mouth is open. Slow breaths wheeze in and out of the channel of my throat; they are the only sound save for the clinking of metal somewhere behind me.

I'm able to move my eyes, though my eyelids are

heavy and obstruct my view. Carver reappears above me, blocking the overhead light. He peels back my right eyelid and purses his lips as he checks for something before removing his hand again.

He begins to sing a tune while wheels scrape over the uneven floor and something hits the right side of the table, reverberating into my arm. I can see the edge of a rolling table, laden with tools.

Fear is alive in my blood. It's screaming in my head as I realize that I *felt* him peel back my eyelid. That I *felt* the rolling cart slap against the wooden table where I'm lying.

That I *will feel* everything he does to me.

Without being able to move.

Without being able to scream.

I was wrong. This isn't the same as what Ford did to me. This is something entirely different. A new form of torture I'll be forced to live through.

Unless…

Unless Carver doesn't mean for me to survive it.

I didn't come this far just to die here in a cold, dank cell that smells of rotting flesh with a demon plucking at my bones.

"Let's have a look inside, shall we?" Carver says with glee before returning to his strange tune, humming and hissing words in a language that's grating to my ears.

The first cut is made to my abdomen. A jagged tearing of flesh that makes my eyes sting and wet croaking sounds burble up my throat in place of a scream. Hot wetness slides over my belly and pools around my wrists.

I'm powerless to stop it when he cuts again, deeper. And deeper still until his blade taps bone, sending a white-hot bolt of searing agony through me.

Inside, I am a symphony of thumping drumbeats and bloodcurdling screams. I am pain incarnate, and I'm not certain I'm still on earth or even still in Elisium.

Because this must be Hell.

It can't possibly be anything else.

"You know," Carver hums, and I roll my head to the side to find him staring into space, his chin propped up on his arms where he rests against my wooden table. His arms covered to the elbow with my blood. "I think you might be one of my best specimens yet."

"Fuck you," I mutter, my mouth still sloppy from his sedative.

My wounds are healing for the third time and the pull and knit of my skin finding its way back together is getting more sluggish each time. As if the pain weren't bad enough, it itches like nothing else I've ever felt in my life. Even poison ivy from that time I tried to run away at five years old wasn't this bad.

I grit my teeth against the maddening sensation, trying to will it away while my body finishes healing.

It's impossible to tell how much time is passing, but he's left twice for long stretches of time to allow me to heal before returning so I assume at least two days.

He grins widely, showing sharp teeth beneath this pale flesh. He's an atrocity. The vilest thing I've ever seen. I hope Kincaid rips out his creepy eyeballs and shoves them down his throat.

Carver leans back and lifts his blood-coated fingers to his lips, licking them with his forked tongue. "Do you know what your blood tastes like?"

I sigh, letting my head roll back, preferring to stare at the ceiling than look at this monster for another second. I don't give him the satisfaction of an answer. I've found that annoys him, and it's the only thing I can do to *not* be cooperative. I think he just likes the sound of his own voice.

When he isn't singing, he tells me things. Awful things. About other's he's *carved*. About how he let them squirm and scream, but that he learned to sedate them so that he could work on them longer. Too much movement and he was bound to hit something important. They died too quickly that way.

"It's sweet," he tells me. "Angel's blood is like that, you know, but you know what's even sweeter?"

I try to picture myself anywhere else, closing my eyes and imagining Kincaid's bed. The soft feel of the sheets. The warmth of his body next to me.

Carver's fist drives down on the table, startling my eyes back open.

"I thought Nephilim at first," he says, exultant. "But I can see now that I was wrong."

He rises to pace the floor, his long nails scratching at his chin.

"The blood of a demon runs in your veins, too. Both lines pure."

He grunts, stopping to swipe the tools from his cart, letting them fall to clatter on the stone floor, cutting himself in the process. The wound oozes with a sickly black ichor instead of blood.

The Carver bellows, swiping the ichor away and bashing the metal cart into the wall. His bulging eyes are crazed when he looks at me next, and despite my attempts to show him none of the fear I feel within, I squirm at the look he gives me.

"It's not possible," he spits, his hunched back heaving with rapid breaths. He pounds on the sides of his head. "*Think!*"

My chest goes cold and a layer of sweat beads on the rounded tops of my breasts. I'm not naked, but I might as well be, with only my panties and socks on, and I'm guessing I only have those still because Carver was too lazy to take them off.

"Unless…"

His voice trails off in a hiss, and I gulp when he slides back to the table, leveling himself next to my face with incredulous eyes.

"Unless what?" I can't help myself. The pain in my ribcage where Carver notched out a section of bone hours ago is healed enough now that I feel I can speak.

"We'll have to look inside to be sure," he says

without answering me, rising once more to continue the conversation with himself, as though I am not even here. "Inside the womb, *yes*. And inside the mind, but we'll save that for last, little flower."

He rubs his tacky hands together and begins to gather up his things from the floor, dumping them back onto the workbench before he rights the cart.

"My lord will be so pleased," he proclaims to himself in a whisper, and it's those six words that force my sluggish mind back to working.

I crane my neck to see him, wincing when the movement sends a ricochet of slicing pain up through my spine. "Who?" I ask, but he's still muttering to himself and my voice is weak. Inaudible against the rattle of his tools as he arranges them in a neat row to wash.

"Which lord do you work for?"

I cough, tasting new blood on my tongue as my body convulses with each racking spasm and my breaths begin to sound strained. Wheezing.

I'd already relegated myself to the knowledge that eventually, my body wouldn't be able to come back from what Carver did to it, but now, if he planned to mess with my brain, I knew that was the endgame.

Not even a being with the blood of both a demon and angel running through their veins would survive that. And that was assuming this psychopath was right.

When he turns back to me with a sharp scalpel pinched between his fingers, I flinch. He should be done. He usually leaves after a few hours of his morbid work. He can't start again.

I can't take it.

"Please," I beg. "No more."

He smiles down at me with the sort of smile you might give a very cute, but very *daft* child. A piteous thing of strained eyes and a wicked lifting of the lips. "Oh, my little flower, we've only just begun."

He drags a chair to the side of the table and sets down his trusty mortar next to my head. I press my lips firmly shut, breathing like a cornered bull from only my nose. But he doesn't shove the awful mixture down my throat.

Carver lifts a piece of my grimy hair from the wooden table and slices through it, tossing the strands into the mortar. To that he adds a few drops of shimmery white liquid from a vial and begins to mash and scrape.

I know better than to think this means I'm safe. He does this sometimes. Taking a piece of skin or hair or bone to see how it reacts with other substances. It means a reprieve only. And usually not for very long.

"With your eyes, I'll make a spyglass," he tells me with a cheery tone as his tongue slips out between his lips and he bites down on it with the effort of grinding up the mixture in his gray mortar. "A spyglass to see the realm of spirits."

He blinks at me and then frowns. I wonder if he is

expecting praise for the announcement. He certainly isn't going to get that from me.

"You wouldn't know any of my work, would you?" he sneers, rolling the pestle around before lifting the mortar to his lips for a taste. I cringe.

He cuts off some more of my hair and adds it to the bowl, resuming his grinding work. "A pity, for then you would understand just how important you are. You see, little flower, I make fantastic things with my carvings. A mirror that can show a fondest memory. A fine powder of gargoyle bone that can turn the skin to stone. Even a key that once opened the gates to Hell."

"A Scepter?" I ask, my voice cracking.

He goes still, tipping his head until his eyes are trained on me, calculating. "So, you do know my work. Tell me, flower, where is my Spirit Scepter? I should like to see it again."

I close my mouth. *Not a fucking chance I'm leading you straight to Art, Devereaux, and Tori, you piece of shit.*

"Very well, keep that secret. My Lord Lucifer has its twin. Though I should think that what I can make him out of *your* carving will render its predecessors obsolete."

"*Lucifer*," I breathe, a new kind of fear taking root in what he's implying. What it would mean for Kincaid if Carver was working for the devil. If *he* was the one ripping the souls from the celestial bodies of The Seven.

If that were true, then I needn't worry about

Kincaid and the others killing each other over my absence. He was as good as dead. We all were.

"Imagine the possibilities," Carver whispers reverently, pausing to stare into the distance. "I could craft him a staff that would not only aid in the removal of souls, but could also cause their immortal destruction. One that would not require the sway of the twin moons to magnify its power."

I gasp, the sound choking off into a sob at his admission.

I can't let that happen. I can't let him take from me what he needs to create such a weapon.

"My lord would forgive me, I think, even if he did find out where the carving came from."

I need to warn Kincaid. I have to get out. I have to get free.

The Carver tips the mortar to his lips again and rolls the liquid around on his tongue before spitting it onto the floor and swiping the back of his hand over his lips.

Then, seeming to get a new idea, he abandons the mortar in favor of a very familiar device. The baton is long, ribbed, and black. He hasn't turned it on yet, but when he does, thin blue wires of pure electricity will jump from one copper prong to the other at its tip.

It will burn and sting when he jabs it into my flesh.

My vision will go black while it wreaks havoc on my nerve endings.

I seal my eyes shut and hold my breath, waiting, but

he forces them back open and I shout, screeching as he fixes bits of silver metal to my eyes, some sort of device that keeps them open no matter how hard I try to force them closed.

Carver positions himself above me, and I feel my skin flay open at my wrists and ankles when I pull too hard against the binds, making the whole wooden table beneath me wobble with the force of my struggle.

He looks emotionlessly into my eyes as he jabs me. The prod switches on with a crackle, and he punches me in the stomach with it. Every inch of my body tightens and burns as a froth churns in my mouth, spilling over my lips while my vision blackens.

I don't realize I've pissed myself until the prod is removed and I twist my head to vomit down the side of the table.

"Hmm."

I haven't even regained my breath, my eyes burning like they're about to burst into flame before he moves in for round two.

24

We're back at The Freakshow.

Or at least, it's where The Freakshow used to be. Now, it's a burning wasteland. Smoke burns my eyes and permeates the air, getting clogged in my throat. That doesn't matter, though.

Kincaid has his arms around me and I can't think of any place I'd rather be than standing amid the wreckage at his side. His hands stroke my hair and curl tightly around my middle, keeping me close.

Keeping me safe.

"Can we go home?" I ask him, my voice an echo of sound, like we're in a vacuum chamber instead of on solid ground. A sob grows in my chest, and I tremble as it passes my lips, knowing and wishing I didn't, that this is a dream.

Instead, I pretend. I inhale his hickory and musk

scent and clench my fists into his jacket. Maybe if I just hold tight enough, I'll be able to stay here, in this dream, as Carver removes my brain from my skull.

"There is no home for us, *Na'vazēm,*" he replies in a gruff rumble. "Not anymore."

But he's wrong. I try to tell him so, but he just squeezes me tighter. Constricting until I can barely breathe. Kin...*Kincaid,*" I eek out through the crushing force around my middle. But he only uses more force. "*Kincaid!*"

My ribs creak, on the verge of breaking.

And then we're gone.

No, we're here.

At the top of a tower on a terrace of stone bricks, looking out into an abyss of misery and coiling flame.

It's HighTower.

Kincaid's kingdom in Hell.

The blistering heat scorches my cheeks as he releases me, his face a sorrowful thing that it hurts me to bear witness to.

"Don't give up," I urge him, grabbing his face between my palms. "We can save you," I promise him. "Just take us home!"

"Save me?" he asks, shaking his head slowly. I hate the lack of emotion in his voice. I hate the flat tone of it. The helpless plea buried beneath its surface. "No, *Na'vazēm,* I cannot be saved. I do not *want* to be saved."

I slap him, and his head jars to one side, but he doesn't even flinch at the strike. "Don't say that."

"I couldn't even save you. *I couldn't even find you.*"

Rage pools like acid in his eyes, turning them electric in the hazy gray space between us. His demon form presses against the sheath of his clothes, making them tear as the inky blackness spreads and his horns grow.

My lips part as he lifts himself up, towering above me like the monster he is. Except, he isn't that. Not really.

I wish I'd seen it before like I can see it now. He's…beautiful.

A breathtaking composition of strength and ferocity. Every hill and valley of ash-black skin is without flaw. His dark horns are shot through with bits of silver, as though they contain the night sky within their beveled edges. His eyes are purest gold in a face that would bring even an angel to their knees.

His pain is almost too much for me to bear.

I set an unsteady hand on his chest, feeling the hard beating of his demon heart pump against the ridges of my palm. "You *did* find me," I whisper. "I'm here."

He softens under my touch, and when he drops his head, I press my mouth to his. His enlarged arms wrap around me, lifting so that he can kiss me more easily. When my hands trail over his horns, he shudders, moaning against my lips, forcing them open, so that he can delve in with his tongue.

He steals all rational thought away, and I revel in his kiss. In the nearness of him. In how *real* it feels to be here. He only pulls away when the saltiness of my tears reaches our joined lips.

"Na'vazēm," he murmurs, swiping a dark thumb beneath my eye. "What is it?"

"I," I start but choke off on a sob. "I wish this was real."

He pulls back as though shocked, holding me at arm's length. His eyes are wide and wild. "Paige?"

An earth-shattering agony rips through my core, and I tip my head back in a scream, clutching my hands to my chest to try to stop it.

"Paige!" Kincaid roars, shaking me.

The last thing I see before I'm ripped from his arms is a curl of black smoke where Kincaid had been standing.

"Fascinating," Carver raves. "Where did you go just now?"

I stare down in horror at the metal tools keeping my chest cavity open to the stinging air. I squeeze my eyes shut when they catch sight of my beating heart, exposed to the air. I can move this time, and Carver must have needed me to remain asleep while he worked on me because other than a vague tingle and the sting of the air, I feel only a displaced sort of feeling.

A pressure. The pressure of his tools keeping my body from healing itself while he watches my internal organs function.

Even though I can move, just barely, I do not try. Afraid that if I do, my heart could be punctured.

"Your heart," he points, and I open my eyes but do not dare look. "The rhythm changed, and your eyes turned black all the way to the edges."

What?

I'm trying to hear what he's saying but I can't focus, my mind reeling and whirling on the fact that my body is broken. My organs are exposed. *My heart is right there.* All it would take is one little poke and he could stop its erratic pulsing for good.

Oh god.

"You traveled, didn't you?" he asks. "Did you visit another dreamer? Asmodeus? Is he still alive, then?"

I...traveled? "Wh-what?"

"Did you give him any clue of where we are?"

Carver's tongue slides over his dry lips as he taps a blood-coated tool against his chin. "Suppose we'll have to speed up the process. Just to be safe."

He turns and walks away, shucking off long plastic gloves and discarding them into a trash bin next to his work bench. "I hadn't expected you to be able to slip free of your mind this far underground. My mistake."

The gravity of what he's saying hits me like a speeding truck.

It was some sort of out of body experience. I'd jumped into Kincaid's mind. Into *his* dream. I was really there. Really with him. And instead of *using* that, I squandered it.

Those were the last moments I'd ever spend with him and I *wasted* them.

I want to pull at the binds and scream bloody murder and thrash until my skin tears and my bones snap. I want to slam my body around until one of Carver's tools does puncture my heart, purely on the hope that he can't do anything with my corpse. Maybe then Kincaid would be safer?

I don't do any of that though. I sit in prone silence while hot tears steam down the sides of my face, a gaping emptiness consuming me from the inside out.

I had a chance…

A chance to tell him who has me. What my cell looks like.

A chance to tell him I'm sorry.

To say goodbye.

And I just stood there like an idiot, happy to be lost to a dream of my demon. Naive. *Useless.*

I am all of the things Ford said I was and more.

"Tomorrow," Carver hisses from somewhere behind me, but I haven't the energy or the care to even bother looking. "Tomorrow I'll open up your skull and begin the carving. *Yes*. Tomorrow."

A cold laugh rises up my throat, and I let my body sag against the table. Would it be a fool's hope to pray that whatever ability I tapped into in my sleep would manifest itself a second time?

My jaw is pried open and something small and round is dropped into my throat. Carver holds his hand to my mouth and pinches my nose until I *inhale* whatever it is he's stuffed into my mouth. I choke and splutter, but it's beyond regurgitating.

The haze sets in almost straight away, and I feel my eyelids begin to close. My pulse steadies. Carver's hideous face distorts, the world tips sideways, and I remember something Ford used to say: There might not be a tomorrow for you, girl. Be grateful I've given you today.

I wish he would have made good on that threat. Then I wouldn't be here. Then I wouldn't have to feel the pain of knowing that Kincaid might soon be sentenced to an eternity in the black void where his brothers waste away. Leaving Artemis alone and undefended. Who would take care of him when we were both gone? Who would get Lady Devereaux home and stop Tori from going after Tristane with a butter knife and pure rage?

What is it they say? Better to have loved and lost than never to have loved at all?

Yeah. I can't say I agree.

Love, I think, is the worst emotion of all.

25

Carver hasn't returned, and it's been hours since I woke. I've tried to force myself back asleep—to try to reach Kincaid again without whatever Carver gave me last night blocking my attempts. But it turns out when you know you have only hours to live, sleep isn't really a viable option.

I try to conserve energy instead. As useless as it might be to try, this is my last chance to do something, *anything,* to escape. I must have been out cold for at least a full day, unless my healing time has gotten much quicker. There is a puckered pink line of flesh down my middle from where Carver put me back together after his little autopsy, but that's it.

Everything feels like it's where it belongs, and though I'm sore, the pain is manageable and only a mild nausea plagues my stomach. The pangs of starvation long since passed.

I lick my parched lips and twist as best I can to get a good view of the room and anything within reach. There's nothing, of course. If there had been, I'd have tried something already.

Even though I know it's of no use, I inspect the metal clamps around my wrists, pulling gently, but firmly to see if there is any flex at all.

There is none.

I try to dig my fingers into the practically petrified wood table, remembering how I almost ripped out a chunk of the banister at Kincaid's mansion. I am stronger now. I should be able to break the wood apart with my bare hands, but I can't.

Either Carver has given me something to subdue my strength, which would explain the ever-present heaviness in my limbs and fog in my mind, or the thick stone walls surrounding this room also somehow block my strength just as much as they block spirit energy.

I'm guessing the former, but in this strange place, you never know.

I groan. Mentally kicking myself. *There has to be a way out.*

This can't be *it*.

What if it isn't?

I'm Diablim. I'll go to Hell, won't I?

A vision of the swirling column of fire carrying naked souls down into the pit crosses my mind and my stomach turns. But Kincaid would find me there, wouldn't he?

He could save me from eternal damnation. He could spirit me away to HighTower and we could live there. Hot tears burn in my eyes and scape my throat raw. It's a beautiful hope, but I have no idea if it's possible. If he can save me. If I'll even be corporeal on that plane.

...how long he'll survive before Lucifer takes him, too.

At least there was a possibility of my being able to warn him. If he could find my spirit in the underworld.

Footsteps outside in the hall spur my heartbeat into a sprint and despite the futility of it, I pull at my binds again, creating new lacerations on my wrists and ankles.

The coded door beeps before swinging open, and I arch myself to see Carver enter, carrying an armful of new tools and devices.

Before the door swings shut, something plucks at my core. The tiniest of spiritual tugs. I think maybe I've imagined it, but it comes again, just once before the door shuts completely and the tugging halts.

There's someone out there.

A person or some kind of spirit. Maybe someone with enough spirit energy that I can draw on it.

Carver hums to himself as he places several tools atop his rolling cart, being even more precise than usual. A dark gray smock is tied around his middle and his sagging neck. He adds a hammer to the cart last and then wheels it over.

"Can I," I stammer, blurting the words. "Can I have a drink? Some whiskey or something."

He cocks his head at me, beady eyes narrowing.

"As a last request," I add, hoping to appeal to any shred of human decency the monster may still possess. "Please."

I need him to open that door.

He studies me for a moment before going back to the task at hand, lifting a thick leather strap with silver eyelet holes on either side and laying it over my forehead. I shake my head and it falls off, making him snarl at me.

"Remain still."

"No. I just want a fucking drink."

"And you'll not get one. I will not have my specimen clouded by any substance."

That was why he was using a strap, I realized, cold dread pooling in my belly. He wasn't going to drug me. Not this time. He couldn't if he wanted an untainted view inside my head.

"I won't risk your fine bones not taking to my carving, little flower. Now *hold still*. It'll be over very soon."

I thrash my head about, not letting him get the strap into place. It slides over the sweat-slicked pane of my forehead again and again each time he tries.

With a hiss, he slaps the leather strap down on the wood and snaps his fingers. Two of his scalpels whizz over as though they've sprouted invisible wings. They settle into place next to my ears, one gets a little too close, nicking the surface and making a droplet of warm blood fill the cavity.

I flinch and only manage to cut open my other ear.

I can't move.

If I do, I'll wind up driving one of these scalpels into my head.

I guess now I knew what sent Isolde flying into the piece of rebar in the tunnel beneath the old church. Carver did. With his telekinetic ability. As if the fucker needed any more reasons to be creepy, he's also a living, breathing demonic poltergeist.

"You fucking bastard," I spit through gritted teeth as he lays the strap over my forehead triumphantly and sets the first nail in the eyelet, pounding it in with the hammer until I think I might go deaf.

He resumes humming to himself as though I'm not practically frothing at the mouth with rage. My muscles are tense and hot and my chest aches from the pounding of my heart.

When he finishes with the first nail in the left side, he chooses another and moves to the right, pulling the strap as tight as it will go. For a second, I wonder if I'd rather impale myself on his hovering scalpels then let him carve me up. I think I would.

I brace myself, ready to jerk my head to the side and hope the scalpel is able to get as far in as it needs in order to make sure I don't survive. If a bit of whiskey could mess with Carver's plans, then I was willing to bet my original theory was correct. If I died before he could carve me up, then he wouldn't be able to do what he wanted with my bones.

I'm sorry, Kincaid.

Carver lifts the hammer over the head of the nail, ready to swing. I have to be faster. I hesitate and a strangled cry lifts from my lips. He stops short and I peel one eyelid back to find him with a confused scowl on his face, head tilted to the side, listening for something.

I strain to hear over the blood rushing in my ears, but after a second, I think I can hear it, too. Scratching. An odd tinny noise like…

Like tiny claws scratching at a metal door.

Carver sets down the hammer and discards the nail. I hold my breath.

Please.

I reach out with my mental feelers, shaking all over.

Please.

Carver presses four buttons on the keypad. It chirps and the door opens.

A startled grunt sounds and the scalpels drop, clattering to the table beside my temples. I tip my head, knocking the leather band askew to see. A flash of white darts through Carver's legs and jumps onto the table.

Casper climbs atop my chest, sitting squarely at the center of my breastbone. His green eyes lock on mine as his tail swishes back and forth over my naked belly.

"Damnable creature!" Carver shouts, and I realize there isn't time for shock and surprise.

When Casper lays a paw on my chest and leans in, I realize what he's doing. What he's offering me—*his power.* All I have to do is accept. All I have to do is give up a part of my soul to get it.

"I agree," I say in a breath and then cry out as a fire ignites inside of me. Casper digs his claws in, holding tight while my body convulses until it is done. Until the burning ceases and Casper's eyes glow like twin pools of uranium.

Until my blood buzzes with the vibration of a power so great I fear it might tear me apart from the inside if I do not unleash it.

When Carver lurches toward us, I find his soul. A shriveled, dark thing. Brighter than Kincaid's, but not by much. It's almost slippery as I try to get a hold on it, to grip it in my phantom fist and bend it to my will.

But I'm no master Necromancer. Not yet. And all I manage to do is halt him for an instant while Casper jumps from my chest. I think he's going to attack Carver, but he scurries away like the useless fleabag he is, right to the slow-closing door.

Where a hulking black shape kicks it back open, snapping the hard metal hinges to leave it hanging at an angle.

"Asmodeus," Carver croaks, shucking off my spiritual grip to whir on him, a hand ready at his side. If he snaps those fingers and does anything to hurt Kincaid, I'll cut them off one at a time.

Tori appears behind Kincaid, her violet eyes wide at the sight of me. Her skin stony ashen gray.

"Get her free," Kincaid bellows, rushing in toward Carver.

Tori's hard cold fingers try to work the clamps on my wrists while Kincaid stalks Carver around the table.

"Wait!" I call to Kincaid. There could be more Carver knows, we should take him alive.

"Kincaid!" I shout again, but he's beyond hearing me. He's rage personified. All hard black edges and sharp cat-eyes.

He lunges for Carver, but the demon dodges him, lifting his hands to send a barrage of sharp objects flying at Kincaid. My demon howls as one hits its mark, embedding in his chest, just several inches above his heart. He falls to a knee, hissing.

I struggle to focus, trying to sift through all the energy in the room to get a hold of Carver's soul again. If I can just incapacitate him for *one second* that might be all Kincaid needs.

"I can't get them off," Tori calls, and I don't know if she's telling me or Kincaid as she heaves on the iron bonds, moving to try the ones at my ankles.

Carver's bulging eyes slide over me just as I'm on the verge of taking hold of his soul. His eyes widen, and he lunges at me, hands outstretched like he means to rip my head from my shoulders.

He almost makes it when the sickening sound of bones crunching draws his attention. A monster tears his arm from its socket. A monster with familiar green eyes and a wide mouth set into a noseless face with tall horns jutting up out of its skull.

The monster shoves the dismembered arm down its throat in one gulp before changing form back to a cat. A white cat with the smear of Carver's black blood on the fur around its lips.

Carver stares in muted horror at the grotesquerie of his arm socket. I gag at the sight too, but that isn't what ultimately draws the bile up my throat. It's the *smell.*

Kincaid rises, hot air shimmering around his horns as he closes in on Carver.

I take hold of his soul. Rooting the bastard in place. It's easier this time; he's too much in shock at the loss of his arm to stop me.

Tori grunts, still putting everything she has into trying to pry me free from the table. It's no use. We need the key. "Kincaid," I call in a softer voice, fighting to keep focus on my hold on Carver. "We need to take him alive."

Kincaid's yellow eyes slide my way, fixing on my face for a second before trailing lower to my bare torso. To the slow-healing scar running just beneath my clavicle and all the way down to my belly button.

His face twists at the sight, breaths coming fast and heavy as he turns back to Carver, still twitching and spluttering from my hold on him.

"*No,*" Kincaid growls before he snaps. I turn my head sharply away as Kincaid descends upon Carver. I lose my hold on his soul a moment later but Kincaid doesn't need my help.

Warm blood splatters the side of my face and mostly naked body, turning quickly cold as it drips down my skin. The squelching, guttural sounds of Kincaid unleashing the full wrath of his beast on Carver fill the room, burrowing into my ears.

When I dare part my eyelids, I see Tori at the end of the table, her hands frozen on my binds. Her eyes wide and her skin a sickly shade of green as she watches Kincaid rip Carver to pieces. For the first time, Tori seems genuinely afraid of Kincaid and with good reason.

I'm more than a little shocked he didn't kill her for letting me go. But I am immeasurably grateful that he didn't. Now, she's forced to bear witness to what he could've done to her. What he still might unless I am able to talk him down.

"Tori," I mutter, spitting a bit of rancid black ichor from my mouth. "The keys. Carver has the keys."

Her gaze slides to me, and it takes her a moment to understand what I've just said, still in shock as the awful sounds to my right finally cease.

"I-I can't find them," Tori says a few seconds later,

and bracing myself, I turn, thinking I may be able to spot them.

Kincaid's hands shake as he comes back to himself, the remnants of Carver all around him as though he shoved a hand grenade down the demon's throat.

Tori is toeing pieces of Carver around on the black-streaked floor, using her forearm to shield her nose from the stench.

"Kincaid?"

He has a distant look in his eyes, like he's a million miles away.

"Kincaid?"

His jaw twitches as he flinches away from the name, but he finally comes back to himself, his face breaking at the sight of me.

In two quick strides he's at my side. His blackened fingers take hold of the celestial bind on my right wrist and with brutal force, he breaks it apart. Then leans over and does the same on the other side. The iron cuts into his hands, bright beads of crimson joining the stains of ichor on his palms.

"Got them!" Tori says, rushing to my ankles to undo the binds there while I pull my arms in to my chest, rubbing at the soreness in my wrists and grimacing at the tightness in all of my muscles from being forced to remain still for so long.

Kincaid carefully curves a hand around the back of my neck, slowly lifting me until I'm seated, and he presses his forehead to mine, a shuddering breath leaving his lips. A tightness in my chest draws a sob from my lungs and when my legs come free I bend them, wanting to clutch them to my chest.

Instead, Kincaid guides them to either side of his waist and draws me in until I am flush against the hard plane of his chest. His face burrows into my neck, and his warm breath across my collarbone makes me shiver, remembering how cold I am.

How cold I have been for days.

But that doesn't matter right now. I pull away only enough to see his face. "You're okay."

I didn't realize how terrified I'd been that he might not be. That even if I did manage to escape these four stone walls, I'd be re-entering a world where he may no longer exist. I inspect the wound on his chest, nudging a tattered bit of cloth out of the way. It's already healing, but he's lost a fair amount of blood.

Kincaid's eyes tighten, and his hold on me goes rigid. An entirely different sort of tears prick at my eyes as a line forms between his brows and his demon form retreats, the color returning to his face.

He looks like he might be sick.

"*Na'vazēm...*" he says on a breath, with an almost imperceptible shake of his head. He lifts me from the table, maybe thinking better of whatever he'd been about to say, setting me gently down on my feet.

My knees buckle and I grip the edge of the table to steady myself as Tori rushes over to help steady me even though Kincaid is already there. He cuts her a scathing glare, and she staggers back, hands raised.

"Don't," I tell him. "She's my friend."

His lips press into a hard thin line and even though I want to say more, now isn't the time. I let him sweep me up into his arms even though doing so clearly causes him pain.

Tori shucks off her jacket, and Kincaid pauses to let her drape it over my bare torso.

Thank you, she mouths.

"Rest now," Kincaid murmurs softly, lowering his face to press a kiss on my forehead. His power over my emotion surges into me, bringing a deep sense of luxurious calm that muddies my senses and brings a fog to my mind.

"No," I try to argue, remembering all at once the things I need to tell him. Everything I learned in Carver's dungeon. About Lucifer. About what's happening to the lords. About…me.

"I need to…" My words are slurred and my eyelids droop heavily, obstructing my vision as a tingling begins in my fingers and toes.

"Tell…you…"

"Rest, *Mea Na'vazēm.* Tell me when you wake."

26

"What you're talking about is suicide," Tori's voice floats into my semi-conscious thoughts as I wake. My hand is on my still-naked belly, and I finger the smooth flesh running up my middle. The puckered line of scar tissue is gone, but my eyes haven't yet adjusted enough to see if any mark remains.

"Kincaid, you can't *kill* Tristane. You'll bring the entire angelic armada down on our heads. You know he's the archangel's golden boy."

"Let them come!" Kincaid snaps.

"Fool!" Devereaux chimes in. "You'd bring their wrath down on us all. Your mate would not be spared, Asmodeus. Would you see her dead to appease your fury?"

Something shatters downstairs, and I haul myself

from the edge of sleep, propping my body up as best I can.

"Whoa," Artemis whispers from beside me as they continue to argue downstairs. "Go slow."

"Art!"

My voice is nothing more than a croak, and I clear my throat as I turn, wrapping my arms around him in a fierce hug. I don't know what is happening to me, but I want to cry I'm so glad to see him.

Once, it took days of torment to make me cry. It took eighteen jabs with the prod before I dared let a single tear fall.

What have these people done to me?

I'm falling apart.

"Uh, I'm happy to see you too, but *um...*"

A flush crawls up my neck, and I release him, pulling Kincaid's covers around myself to cover my nakedness. "Sorry."

"All good. I'm glad you're awake. Let me go get Kin—"

Another shattering sound echoes up the stairs, and Artemis sighs.

"How long has that been going on?"

Art shrugs. "Pretty much since they brought you back."

I move to shuffle off the bed, but Artemis stops me with a hand around my arm. "Kincaid said he wanted you to rest. You're still healing."

"I've rested too long already," I all but snap, having

to steady myself with a slow breath to keep from losing my temper. "And Kincaid should have thought of that before he started smashing everything."

I rush to pull on some clothes with clumsy fingers, finding one of Kincaid's discarded tunics on the floor. It goes almost to my knees, and I figure it's good enough. I don't want to waste any more time. Afraid that if I don't intervene, he'll either destroy the entire house or start a war with the angels that we won't be able to win.

Artemis' healing has done wonders on the lingering aches and pains in my bones from Carver's tools, but days without proper food or water keep me unsteady, battling off wave after wave of vertigo as I trudge down the stairs to a cacophony of shouting in the dining room.

Black spots dance at the edges of my vision, but I blink them away, the slow burning fire in my core lighting a fuse that won't be so easily put out.

They silence as I approach, and all eyes turn to me when I enter.

"Paige," Tori exclaims. "You're awake. Are you okay?"

"I will be," I reply as kindly as I can as she pulls out a chair and gestures for me to sit.

I shake my head. I'm too wound up to sit down.

A scattering of broken glass litters the floor at Kincaid's feet. Blood coats his knuckles, but the wounds created when he put his fist through the glass door of the liquor cabinet have already healed. He looks at me like he's seeing a ghost. Like I'm some malicious spirit come to torment him.

His fists clench at his sides.

"You should be resting," he says.

"Ha!" I scoff. "And let you start a war while I sleep? I don't think so."

"Do not insert yourself in matters you do not understand. There must be retribution."

"The angels weren't going to hurt me, Kincaid. Interrogate me, maybe, but not hurt me. And you already got your retribution."

A vivid image of Carver's remains burns itself into my memory and my hand goes to my stomach.

"Go back to bed."

"No."

A muscle jumps in his temple. "You are the most infuriating creature I've ever known."

"Ditto."

Lady Devereaux catches a laugh in her hand, covering the sound with a cough. But then her reflective eyes narrow on me and she steps in, brushing her fingers over my cheek. "What happened?"

What?

"Your soul. It's…different than it was before."

The cause of that little mishap bounds into the room as though called, his little bell jangling. Casper purrs loudly as he moves to rub himself against my legs. I shoo him away with a soft kick. "Go away, you little heathen."

Devereaux looks between the cat and me, understanding softening the crease in her brow.

"He tricked me," I explain. "Got me to accept a trade for power when Kincaid was nearly there."

I kick him away again, more forcefully this time. "And he *could've* just helped me himself. I saw what you turned into. You could have killed Carver all on your own."

Devereaux crosses her arms. "Well, I don't know why you're surprised. He's a trickster demon, after all."

I roll my eyes as Casper hisses at me. "You're lucky I don't make good on my promise to roast you over a spit."

Kincaid glares after the cat as he pads away and there is no doubt in my mind that if our souls weren't linked, he'd be making a kitty kabob himself.

"Anyway, we have more important things to talk about," I say, finding the strength to cut the fuse before I explode. But as my fury wanes, the voices that'd been blocked out from being so far underground resurface, creating the white noise I didn't miss in the back of my head.

"Like what?" Tori asks as Artemis wanders into the room and slumps into a seat. There are dark circles under his eyes and he's paler than a sheet. Kincaid probably had him up all night working on me.

"Like how Carver was in league with the demon responsible for killing Malphas and Dantalion."

I have Kincaid's attention now. He rushes forward, slamming his hands down on the table across from me, fingers splayed. "*Who?*"

I worry how he'll react when I tell him, but there's no avoiding it. Just like I worry there's no escaping death for him if the devil himself is the one dealing it.

"Lucifer."

His lips part as his eyes search mine, perhaps searching for any trace of doubt. He won't find any. I may have blocked out most of what happened down in that dungeon—I may be blocking it still—but that admission is branded into my memory.

"But...why?" Tori asks, falling into the chair she'd pulled out for me, cocking her head. "Why would he kill his own men?"

Kincaid's fingers dig into the mahogany wood of the table, adding gouges to the scrapes already marring the surface. "He has long felt betrayed by us," Kincaid utters, dropping his head as though he's already defeated.

"When the archangels dragged him back to Hell and allowed us to remain as wardens of the damned..."

"He blamed you?"

"He was furious, but not with us. At least, it hadn't seemed that way."

"Then why kill you?" Tori asks, squinting at Kincaid. "What would he have to gain? All he's ensuring by killing the seven is that he'll never have another opportunity to resurface. Without the seven to open the gate, the only beings who could are the archangels, right?"

Kincaid nods gravely.

"Then what's his endgame?" I ask.

"I don't know."

My nails bite into my palms. "We have to stop him."

Kincaid snaps his head up. "No. You will do nothing. I'll not have you in harm's way again, *Na'vazēm.* I will do this alone. If I fail, so be it."

"*Stubborn ass*! You *need* my help. We have to do something," I bark. "If he succeeds, there will be celestial war on earth. Millions will die."

His eyes darken as his gaze slides from my face. "You forget, *Na'vazēm.* I am no hero. I would watch this world burn to keep you safe. And I would do it with a *smile.*"

The room is stunned into silence at his omission, but none more than me. I open my mouth to reply, but find I can't. Someone's hollowed out my insides, shaken up the contents of my mind. Everything's backwards, and I'm not sure how to put it right again. Or that I even want to.

Devereaux wanders closer to the table and Kincaid blinks at her as though he forgot she was even there, but she doesn't notice, her gaze is fixed on me. "Did you learn anything else?"

She's looking at me like she already knows the

answer, and my stomach turns at the thought of admitting it aloud. It seemed inconsequential at the time, but now, faced with Kincaid and Lady Devereaux, I'm not sure what to say.

Will they think of me differently?

It was one thing to have Devereaux speculate about it that night at her cottage in Infernum, but this would only confirm it.

"Yes," I admit after a moment. "But it's not helpful. It doesn't really even matter."

Devereaux looks doubtful as Kincaid rounds the table to me, settling those bright yellow eyes on mine, searching. "What is it?"

I can't look at him. "I...I'm not Diablim. Or at least, not entirely. Carver said—"

"Carver said what?" Kincaid demands and a bolt of alarm races up my spine.

I swallow hard and wet my dry lips before replying, but drawing it out isn't helping anything. "I have angel blood," I admit. "And demon's blood. *Pure,* he said. On both sides."

"That's impossible." Devereaux scoffs.

"I'm just telling you what he said," I sling back at her, heat in my cheeks.

"Angels and demons cannot procreate," Kincaid confirms. "It's been so since the dawning of time."

I grind my teeth. "I'm just tell you what he told—"

"*Wait,*" Kincaid roars, startling me when he grabs

me by the arms, snapping my head up to look at him. "When were you born?"

"What?"

"When were you born?"

I tell him the year, barely able to get the syllables past my lips as panic seeps into my every pore.

"The *date,*" he hisses.

"Kincaid!" Tori shouts, rising like she might try to pry his quickly-blackening hands from my body, but I cast her a warning look.

I manage to wriggle myself out of Kincaid' bruising grip, giving him a withering look. He sobers when he sees the discoloration on my biceps, falling back into the table.

"November," I tell him. "The fourteenth."

"She can't be," Devereaux whispers.

Tori gasps and Artemis drops his head into his hands. What are they all understanding that I'm not?

"Will someone please fucking explain to me what's happening right now? What don't I know?"

"Twenty-three years ago the gates were opened and Lucifer walked the earth," Devereaux mutters to herself and all the breath is robbed from my lungs. My head spins.

Kincaid looks at his hands like they must belong to someone else, and when he lifts his gaze to mine again, I see defeat in the ledger of his stare.

"You're his daughter."

Printed in Great Britain
by Amazon